FIXATED

THE WITCHES OF JACKSON SQUARE

A. LONERGAN

FIXATED

To my mother. Your strength has always defined me and helped me to be better in every aspect of my life. Thank you for being courageous. Without your example, I would have never never had the nerve to fly.

P*ain*

It was all I felt. It left a gaping hole inside my chest. I knew the moment Freya was taken, but with her unconscious, there was no way I was going to be able to track her. I flew around the giant empire that Sariah had created and perched on one of the beams sticking out from the side of it. Vines had wrapped around the metal and exposed beams and almost made the monstrosity look pretty. I closed my eyes and tried to calm my heart and my breathing. The memory had come out of nowhere, and the pain had been renewed.

I had lost her. I had underestimated the witches. I had underestimated Sterling. He was just as devastated as anyone, but he was to blame, unfortunately. He let her get away. A woman alone in the Quarter was enough to raise alarm, but a powerful witch that was wanted? He should have never let her out of his sight. I should have known it was a terrible idea for her to go on a date. Now I was stuck here beating myself up. I shrunk myself down a few more inches and crawled to the wall.

I could hear Sariah screaming. "What do you mean you can't bring me the steel that killed the dragons?"

Queen Armia sighed. "We had it destroyed when my father died."

"There is no one in your kingdom that could recreate it?" I could hear Sariah pacing back and forth.

"No, my father killed the weapons master before they marched to battle. He was too afraid he would create something else even more powerful than himself." Armia sounded annoyed.

"You must figure this out. Their bonding is complete. The only way to keep any damage from happening is to keep them separate." Sariah said matter of fact.

Red hot rage was all I could taste as I grew to the most significant size imaginable. I towered over her little kingdom and lit it up. I no longer cared for the beings that lived within it, I no longer cared for anything. All I felt was anger and fire and pain.

I heard screams and explosions, and I had no doubt that they were going to try to fight me off, but I continued to pour my white fire down on them like the fiery wrath of God. I watched as Sariah ran for her life and I chased after her, I wanted her out of my new city. I wanted her gone for good. There was nothing that I could do to help Freya, but I would take care of the nuisance problem. There was nothing I wouldn't do for my familiar, and this had to be done.

There was a part of me that told me to follow her, that she would lead me to Freya, but I knew the time would come. There was also a tiny bit of fear that Freya was left in the building I had melted to the streets.

CHAPTER ONE

FREYA

My fingers sunk into the mushy ground, desperately searching for something solid to pull me from the marsh. The water was too dense and thick, I couldn't pull my head up for air. My lungs burned, and my head swam as my mind fought to stay conscious.

I made one last attempt as my body started to fade. My foot connected with something solid, and it propelled me from the water. I landed on the uneven marsh and spewed the murky water from my nose and mouth. But before I had any time to recover, I realized I wasn't alone. The sound of movement across the mud was enough to stop me in my tracks. I quickly rubbed my eyes clean and started to move away from the sounds as fast as I possibly could. With every movement, I seemed to sink into the swamp more and more. Finally, the clouds moved away from the moon and lit up the predator in front of me.

The vibrant green eyes were fixated on me. There was no way I was going to be able to escape. The creature was massive, and I was in her territory. The big alligators tail thumped behind her, almost in a warning. My magi warmed my wrist, but it didn't comfort me. It hadn't saved me from nearly drowning in the swamp, what was it going to do now? I had half a mind to rip it from my skin and use it as a distraction.

Distraction.

I tried not to take my eyes away from the beast, but I needed a plan. My magi vibrated against my skin, and I figured it wouldn't hurt to try. I didn't have anything better. I focused on the flat calm water behind the alligator and created a wave. It crashed down on the beast, but instead of running away from me, it made it run toward me. I scrambled up from the mud, my feet slipping and sliding as I barely made it to stand.

I knew that If I continued to look over my shoulder, I was a goner so I focused on the thick woods in front of me and ran as hard and fast as I could. Once I broke through the tree line, a howl cut through the air.

Great.

More predators.

I knew I could possibly outrun an alligator, especially with all these trees, but a wolf? I didn't stand a chance. I didn't slow my pace, but soon the only thing I could hear was my labored breathing and thundering heart.

The sounds of splintering wood were the only thing that stopped me. I put my hand over my heart and turned around slowly. The wolf had crashed into the advancing alligator and knocked it into a tree. Blood dripped from the wolf's muzzle, and its crystal blue eyes bore into mine. It stepped away from the swamp monster and narrowed its intelligent eyes at me before it darted back through the trees. Its light brown fur concealing it as it departed.

I held onto the tree behind me for dear life as the adrenaline started to fade from my body. My legs trembled, and I began to lose my balance. But deep down, I could feel something changing inside me. Before I could pinpoint it, exhaustion began to take hold of me once more, and before I knew it, everything went black.

CHAPTER TWO

STERLING

Freya had been gone for two weeks. She had vanished without a trace. My mother had even roped in the vampires to help search.

Nothing.

It was like she didn't exist.

Ayre had even gone back to her last foster home, but still, no one had seen her. We would have gone to the Mirror Realm if we didn't already know that Queen Armia was on Sariah's side. I felt like I was hitting a brick wall. We had finally found some peace. Vailen had finally driven Sariah out of the Quarter, but it didn't matter. The only reason he did was out of vengeance because he figured she had taken his familiar. There had been blood on the street, but I had also seen her fall before she disappeared. I didn't know if she had run for the high hills because of the drama from Blondie.

"You who is someone around here going to tell me where my daughter is?" Sariah had changed so much in the few weeks since I had last seen her. It was shocking to see her here so soon. Her lips were light blue and dark circles had started to form around her eyes. If I hadn't known better, I would have called her dramatic. I had never seen a dark witch, but I knew the signs. We had been warned about it at the Academy.

"The Awakening has just begun, darling. Don't look so surprised. This is what true magic looks like." She spun around slowly like she was modeling a new look. She wore a ball gown and reminded me of a villain from a Disney princess movie.

"True magic? Really? I'm sure your Magi just loves that." I rolled my eyes.

Sariah smiled wickedly, her teeth looked sharper than they had before. "Oh, my sweet, innocent darling, I don't need one of these wretched things anymore." She pulled the neckline away from her chest and revealed a patch of rotten skin in between her breasts. Black veins were snaking away from it like she had an infection. Though that's probably what it was. The loss of her Magi was poisoning her from the inside out.

"You have no idea the extent of my power." she continued on.

"Then why can't you find your own daughter?" I crossed my arms over my chest. We had assumed she had been responsible. Now I was starting to worry. She rolled her eyes and placed her hands on her hips. Behind her, I could see my mother coming into the courtyard. Her face was void of all emotion.

"I don't need to explain myself to you." She threw her hands around dramatically. "But she is your High Priestess now. Don't you know? Can't you feel it? When your little dragon took my home and forced me out, the transition happened. I'm sure she's not that dumb to not know."

My mother was the one to reply to Sariah. "What has happened to you?" My mother's eyes had filled with moisture.

Sariah turned around slowly to face the one woman she had refused to come to terms with. "Your boy is gorgeous."

My mother shook her head. "You don't get that right. Go back to the swamp."

"I'm looking for my daughter. We have much to

discuss. I would like to be allies for what is coming." For a brief moment, her face relaxed.

"You can't keep her hidden forever. She has responsibilities."

I looked to my mother for guidance. She nodded her head. I licked my lips nervously before I spoke. "She's not here. Something happened a few weeks ago. She was taken."

Sariah's shock seemed genuine. "Taken by whom?"

"We aren't entirely sure. It happened so quickly." I pinched the bridge of my nose, trying my hardest to keep my emotions in check.

"And what was she doing?" She looked at my mother and shook her head.

"The woman who exiled her own daughter wants to play Sheriff now?" my mother said. "You can take your projection and leave now."

Projection? I frowned.

Sariah frowned at my mother's dismissal, but she did as she was told and disappeared.

"I thought she was really here," I said.

"She may no longer be High Priestess, but she is powerful." My mother watched the place Sariah had been, carefully.

"You knew Freya became the High Priestess?" I

asked trying to keep the anger and frustration from my voice.

"I suspected. The powers didn't come back to me, but there has been a shift in the essence." She pulled her hair over her shoulder and turned away from me. "If you had been paying attention, you would have noticed too."

"But why would the essence take the power away from Sariah and give it to Freya if she isn't here? They're both gone." I called after her.

Mom called back over her shoulder. "The essence is full of our ancestors, they know where she is, and they know what we need and what she does. Why they gave Sariah the power back, I don't know, but they do."

I knew all of this, but I just wasn't buying it. Unless Freya was in danger and I prayed that wasn't the case.

CHAPTER THREE

FREYA

I pulled my head from the soft dirt and could barely hear the crickets chirping in the goop surrounding me. I was surprised I had made it through the night. My limbs were heavy, and I had no inkling of where I was.

I pulled myself up and tried to lean against a nearby tree for support. My head swam, and when I looked down at my body, I could have screamed. I was covered in dark purple bruising up and down my legs. My dress was tattered and torn around my waist. I couldn't even tell what color it had been, and I certainly didn't remember.

How long had it been? A few days maybe? There was no way I could have stayed alive in a swamp without food or water for longer than a few days, right? I licked my lips and tasted dried blood and mud. I couldn't imagine how the rest of me looked. My bare feet swooshed and squashed into the soft dirt, and I noticed cuts along the tops of my feet, as well as the bottom. I cringed as I walked, sharp pains shot up my ankles and into my legs.

I shivered against the cold morning dew that was stuck to my skin. I wrapped my arms around myself and ambled through the wooded marsh. The last thing I remembered was getting hit on the head after everything had happened with Sterling and then the wildly vivid memory from Vailen. Something snagged my hair, and I was pulled backward. I tried to swat it away, but no matter how hard I worked, I couldn't go.

When I turned around to free myself from the suspected branch, my breath got stuck in my throat. It was no branch that was holding onto my matted, mucky hair. It was a creature from children's nightmares. It was everything the cajun Mawmaw's warned you about in their bedtime stories. The beast almost resembled a werewolf but was more twisted. Its mouth hung open slightly, and where it was supposed to have eyes, there were just sockets.

Its arms were bent at odd angles, as well as its legs. Its head looked like it had been stretched by something. The thing towered over me by at least three feet. His foul breath huffed into my face. Bile rose up my throat at the smell.

The rougarou growled deep within its throat and bent forward to take a long sniff. Too afraid of what was to happen next, I put my hands out, and power flew from me like never before. I felt some of my hair rip from my skull, but as soon as I was free from the beast, I took off running. Sticks and gumballs dug into my feet, but I didn't stop. I didn't care to even look back to where he had landed. Fear and adrenaline pumped double time through my veins. When I made it to more water, I stopped and caught my breath. There was nowhere else for me to go.

I looked around me and spun in a circle, not wanting to be taken by surprise again. Pain lit up through my head, and I doubled over. Pressure pushed on my limbs and caused me to fall to my aching knees. Dizziness overtook me, and I found myself unconscious once again.

BACK ON THE SWAMP FLOOR.

I blinked against the dirt, my eyelashes fanning the soft terrain. The pain was still there but wasn't as bad as before. At least the monster wasn't back to finish me off.

When I sat up, it was almost as if I was looking through new eyes. The world was much more vibrant than before and based on the placement of the sun, I didn't think much time had passed. But who was I kidding? We had never been taught survival in skills in school.

It was almost as if my senses were heightened or in overdrive. I blinked a few more times and rubbed the crusted dirt from my face.

High Priestess... A whisper.

Chosen one... Another whisper.

Freya...

I looked around the woods frantically. I had no idea where the whispers were coming from, but they were starting to creep me out.

Plan.

I needed a plan. I was surrounded by water and monsters of every caliber.

"Child don't be afraid. Please." A thick Cajun accent washed over me.

I was getting really tired of the voices. I covered my ears with my hands, and because of that, I missed the sound of movements from a real human. When the older woman stepped into my sight, I jumped.

Her smile was sympathetic. Her youthful, ebony skin glistened, and I secretly wanted to know how she looked so amazing in this swampy terrain. The only indication that the woman was over thirty was her gray dreads. They were pulled away from her face in a tight bun.

I removed my hands from my ears and scooted away from her. Sometimes looks were deceiving.

"There's nothing to be afraid of." The same Cajun accent hit me again. It was soothing to listen to.

"How did you find me?" I gulped hard. My magic had protected me earlier, but would it be up for the task again? My magi was calm, so that was a good sign.

"I didn't, one of our scouts last night reported seeing you," she spoke carefully.

I nodded my head trying to remember the night before. The wolf and the alligator... I looked around. There was no way I had run that far away from the mess. But everywhere I turned, it all looked the same, and there was no dead gator or a busted up tree.

"Do you remember what happened to you?" The woman crouched low in front of me. Her bright blue eyes assessed my body. They seemed eerily familiar.

"I was kidnapped from my cove- " I cut myself off. Judging by the color of her eyes she wasn't a witch. Her eyes cut down my body again, and her eyebrow quirked when she eyed my Magi.

I started again, "I was kidnapped and dumped here. I woke up struggling in the swamp."

"Can I bring you back to our camp? We have a doctor that lives next door, and I'm sure he wouldn't mind looking you over." She held her hand out to me. "I'm Agata."

I found myself taking her hand and letting her support some of my weight. Now that the adrenaline had worn off, I realized that my ankle was severely messed up and putting pressure on it was almost impossible.

A chill raced up my body and made me stumble. "You're alright now, little witch. We're going to get you back to your coven." Her words stopped me. I could feel my heart rate pick up and I looked around for a place to run. "I'm not here to harm you, but based on some observing, I'm going to take it, you either have memory loss from your trauma or your Sariah's daughter back from the dead." Her blue eyes bore into mine.

CHAPTER FOUR

STERLING

I paced the floor. Vailen was still gone. He had been gone for a week after Sariah had popped in, he had said that he felt her, for the first time since Freya had been gone. Hope had swelled within me. Now dread had taken its place.

"Calm down. I know you're anxious. But it'll do you no good to wear a hole in the floor." Shay said from my bed. She was perched on the corner watching me with a worried expression.

"I can't, I feel like I'm going to burst at any moment." I stopped and scrubbed my hands down my face.

Shay's eyebrows wrinkled. "Look, I understand you feel responsible, but this isn't your fault."

"But it is. Every time this has happened, I

played a part in it." I shoved my hands into my suit pant pockets.

"Sterling, I don't understand your obsession." She rolled her eyes. "Yes, I understand that she's your High Priestess, but she's not *that* special."

My mouth went dry, and I immediately felt regret for trying to get close to her. I regretted the kiss we had shared and glad that it hadn't gone farther than that. I shook my head, no thoughts came to my mind, and I had no idea how to react. All I could do was turn on my heel and leave the room.

I thought on her words and got sick to my stomach. Not that special? I had come to understand that there was something special about everyone and to say that she wasn't that special bothered me to my core. I had learned too much in the past few months just to let Shay get in my head and turn me back to the person I had been before. The person that hadn't cared about anything but politics in the council and ass.

I pushed my hair from my forehead and bumped into someone. When I looked up, I came face to face with my sister.

"What is Shay doing in your room?" She shoved her finger into my chest, angrily. "Didn't you go on a date with Freya? I thought you had feelings for her?"

"That's not what's going on. " I looked at her confused. "I don't exactly know how I feel about Freya, but she's not here for me to figure that out."

"So you went ahead and started to move on? Oh yeah, she'll understand that when she gets back." Ayre rolled her eyes.

I sighed. "The date didn't exactly end well."

She folded her arms over her chest. "This is a story I haven't heard yet."

"An old fling of mine came to the restaurant, though after Freya left, the girl looked confused and asked where she was." I had been keeping the story to myself, afraid to start anything, especially with Vailen out of sorts.

Ayre gasped. "Compulsion?" Her facial expression started to change as she figured what all this meant. "Vampires. Mom called in the Vampires, but they aren't loyal?"

I covered her mouth with my hand and pulled her into the shadows. "You shouldn't speak such things. At least, not out loud."

Her eyes got wide, and she nodded her head. I removed my hand from her lips and stepped back. I looked around the hallway to make sure all was clear.

"There are people here that don't agree with Freya being put into a position of power, but more than that, they don't agree with Freya being here at all." I considered my words carefully. "She is the daughter of a traitor. They are worried about where her loyalties lie."

She closed her eyes, and her face went grim. "You'll need to do a truth serum on Liam."

Now that she understood what was happening, she knew she couldn't protect anyone, especially her crush if we wanted to find Freya. There was pain in her eyes, but she was loyal to what was right. I put my hand on her shoulder and yanked her close to me.

I whispered an incantation, and blue electricity erupted around us. The only reason Ayre could see it was because I was touching her.

"We are no longer alone." I didn't worry about whispering. The spell would protect our words between us. "You can't trust anyone."

Her eyes looked around frantically, searching for the intruder. The only reason I knew there was one, was because of my Magi. Before I had whispered the spell, my Magi had lit up against my chest, like I had been zapped with electricity.

"I'm not allowed to do the truth serum, but if Father summons Liam, he'll run." I scratched my head. I was stuck. I didn't know what I was to do. If I went to father and told him what was happening, the silent intruder would know and warn the rebellion.

We had suspected a rebellion when Liam had risen up in the courtyard. But now that we had our heads put together, I knew there was more to this than what we knew. I had heard whispers the last few days and was worried something would happen at any moment.

"Sterling?" Shay's voice echoed down the hall, and I felt dread and suspicion toward her. Her sudden appearance couldn't be coincidental. "I'm sorry, I didn't mean what I said."

Her voice grew closer, and Ayre shook her head. "Drop the spell." When the spell was gone, she whispered loudly, "She doesn't sound very sincere."

Shay popped her head into the space beside us, and she gave Ayre a dirty look. "I am sincere."

Ayre obviously and openly didn't like her. "Ha, and I'm a vampire."

Shay turned toward her with a look of surprise.

Ayre stuck her tongue out and retreated. This wasn't over. I knew my sister, and she loved revenge. She was not happy that our conversation had been interrupted. She wanted to be in the know and hated being left in the dark. She often was too. Father and I were afraid she had inherited too much of mom's air-headedness. When it came down to it, she was better off not knowing.

Shay pouted in front of me. "Why be so secretive? There's no need to hide."

I played along and let her thread her fingers through mine. "She was asking about us." The lie spilled from my lips easily.

I had always been a good liar, and the smile that lit up Shay's face just confirmed it.

CHAPTER FIVE

FREYA

U *gh.*

Not again.

I woke up alone and cold, but this time I was restrained. I just couldn't catch a break.

"Finally, we were starting to worry that we would have to send our little friend away," Agata said from the corner of the dim room. Her face was a mask of disappointment.

I pulled my wrists and tried to free them, but no such luck. Whatever was binding me to the chair was powerful magic. I tugged at my binds a few times, but all it did was send pain racing up my shoulders. I let my arms relax, trying to get comfortable. There was no doubt in my mind that I would be here for a while and having your arms bound behind your back wasn't the most pleasant experience.

I just stared at the woman and didn't say a word. Her icy blue eyes practically glowed in the dark. "Come in!" she called.

The door opened, and a figure in a black cloak came in. From what I could tell, it was dark outside. I slumped my shoulders. More time lost.

"Don't move." The voice sounded scratchy, almost like they had used a spell to disrupt the sound. The cloaked person pulled something from the pocket on the side of the cloak. I could tell from the persons delicate hands that it was probably a woman, but I didn't see much else as she went behind me. Her steps were heavy and slow.

I felt a prick at my neck, and I jerked forward. The chair lifted onto its front legs, where my ankles were bound, and I toppled over. My head smacked the floor and tears clouded my vision. I swallowed back a cry and bit my tongue.

"There's no need for violence. Our pack only has a few questions, no need for it to escalate." Agata said through gritted teeth.

"A truth serum is a powerful force to yield.

What happens once it has been initiated isn't me. It's the magic." The hooded figure said, now crouching beside my head.

Chills erupted all over my body and pain was crawling up the back of my neck. Whatever she had done was starting to work. It felt like little needles stabbing my scalp. I let out a whimper but wanted to remain strong. I didn't want to be broken so easily.

"What's your name?" Agata said.

My reply was automatic, almost robotic. "Freya Coilette."

"Who is your mother?" she asked.

"I don't have one." The reply was more me this time. Fiery hot pain lit up my arms until I muttered, "Sariah Coilette."

"Why are you in our bayou?"

"I was kidnapped a few days ago, and I can't remember what happened after that." My words came out quickly.

"Where is your mother now?"

"Probably in her kingdom she built in the business district." I stopped trying to pick my head up and laid it on the dusty wooden floors. It was too dark in the room to make out anything distinguishable.

"Are you working with your mother?"

I laughed, short and harshly. "Never in my life would I work for or with her."

"What is your relationship with Sterling Masters?"

Dread licked up my spine. A question I didn't want to answer at all. I bit my tongue to keep myself from spilling all my feelings and secrets. Pain burst on my wrist where my magi was. I tried to separate my hands to help with the pain. It was no use, I now knew how the truth serum worked. My poor magi would be tortured if I didn't answer correctly or at all. I continued to hold my tongue until I felt the first little leg break from my skin.

The sound of metal clanging against the floor was defining, and the pain that followed was unlike anything I had ever experienced. I let out a shriek and tried my hardest to pull free. I threw my body around in hopes I would break the chair.

The hooded figure repeated Agata's question. "Who is Sterling Masters to you?"

"He was mean to me. He treated me poorly. I tried to avoid him at all costs." The words hurt coming out, my magi knew the truth and would be punished. I clenched my teeth together and squeezed my eyes closed as another leg dropped from my wrist, and it felt like I was on fire. Sweat broke out all over my body, and if I continued like this, I would have bitten my tongue off.

"Answer the question," Agata said gently from her dark corner. "We don't want to hurt you."

My eyes flew open, and I let out a laugh that didn't even sound like me. "I don't want anything to do with him. I liked him, and he's nothing but a player."

The pain eased, and I was surprised by the truth my mouth had spoken, especially when I was delirious from the pain and didn't even form the sentence myself. My mind was a muddled mess, and I couldn't focus on a certain word or even form a coherent thought.

"Interesting," Agata said. "Is your brother alive?"

"I don't know." I groaned. My head spun, and my vision went dark. My stomach growled, and it sounded like an angry cat. I didn't know the last time I had eaten or drank.

"Is it true that you are the High Priestess now?"

"I don't know. I don't think so." I licked my dry lips and closed my eyes.

"I think we are done here," Agata told the hooded person.

"Because she held back information, her magi will continue to punish her. She'll probably be here for hours." The mystery person pushed through the door and left.

"Why did you hold back information if you knew this would happen with the truth serum?" Agata whispered. She knelt down beside me.

"I didn't. I didn't know what a truth serum was before today." This was something I would never forget now.

Agata swore. "She told me you knew, she told me you had been informed on what a truth serum did. I- I didn't mean to cause you harm or pain. I just needed answers before you came to my pack. Most beings do this to protect their families."

I nodded my head against the ground. "Will you undo the magic binding me?"

Her fingers elongated, and she slashed through the magical bonds. I was too tired to think of how or why it worked. I wanted to stretch, but my body was too weak to do so.

Agata helped me roll onto my back. "The healer is coming to help you get comfortable, and he'll bring food."

She leaned in closer, and I had just enough energy to wrap my fingers around her neck. Agata's eyes held sadness, and she didn't fight me. She allowed me to squeeze until I just let go of her. She stumbled backward and held her head high. She didn't say anything, and when someone knocked on the door, she fled.

An older man approached me. He had a steaming tray, but I couldn't tell what the contents were. He appeared to be in his 80's, and his bright blue eyes seemed to see right through me.

"Agata means well," he said with a thick French accent. "She's worried about her people."

I could understand that. I had deserved a warning from the witch though. I also wanted to know the identity of the witch, but I knew I wouldn't get much from these people.

A wave of pain crashed into me, and I curled up into a ball. I cried out and tried to fight it, but it only made it worse. Wave after wave hit me like electricity. It thrummed through my body and made me gasp.

The healer sat beside me and rubbed circles on my back, trying to soothe and comfort me. My body shook violently from the shock of it all. The shaking finally stopped, and I laid there on the wood floor, trying desperately to collect myself.

My hands trembled as I pushed my damp hair away from my face. My body was coated in sweat, and I couldn't tell if I had soiled myself.

The healer pulled my hands and helped me sit up just enough so he could slide a pillow under my shoulders. He held up a cup to my lips, and the bitter taste made me choke. The warm liquid dribbled down my chin, but I made no move to wipe it away.

"You must drink, it will help with the truth serum." He urged me to take another sip, and I struggled to swallow it down, but I did it.

Sure enough, after a few minutes, the trembling went away, and I felt somewhat better. The only thing covering my body was a thin sheet, and I distinctly remembered my appearance when I had woken up in the swamp.

I was in no position for favors. I kicked the chair away from me and pulled the sheet around myself. The healer stared into nothing and sat there motionless. I knew that if I wanted to, I could escape, but where to? Another area in the swamp? In the middle of a town? By the looks of the worn wooden cabin, I doubted I was near civilization.

I pushed my fingers through my matted hair.

The healer finally looked my way. "I'll go get the materials to treat your legs and the rest of your bruised body."

I nodded a thank you, and he was gone.

CHAPTER SIX

STERLING

It had been another two days. I knew I shouldn't have let him go alone. My mother observed me from across the room. I tried to keep my attitude in check. I didn't want her to suspect anything. I didn't want to keep my mom out of the loop, but I knew I needed to. Ayre grabbed my hand under The table and squeezed. Mom narrowed her eyes at us. She knew us better than anyone. Absent from the table was Shay and Liam. Lately, my father had started doing formal meals. He was suspicious of the witches that never attended them. Shay and Liam had both only attended one.

I pushed away from the table and nodded at my father. He knew more than he let on. How else would I have gotten my hands on the ingredients to make a truth serum? I had found them in my father's unlocked desk. Which was unheard of. He was never irresponsible unless he was allowing things to happen. He didn't want Liam to know he suspected him, so he was letting me sneak. At least that's what I thought. If my father called for someone to have a truth serum, everyone would know it. We wanted this under the radar as much as we could get it.

I could feel Ayre's eyes on my back as I left the dining room. She knew exactly what I was about to do. I didn't have a plan per se. I just knew I needed to act fast. I walked with steadfast purpose to Liam's room. I rasped my knuckles against the wood and waited.

Finally, the door swung open. I played the angry brother role. His hair was standing up around his head, and his polo shirt was unbuttoned.

He shot a nervous smile my way and leaned against the door frame. "What can I do for you, Sterling? Ole daddio ain't mad I missed his little dinner?"

"No, that's not why I'm here." Showtime. I pinched the bridge of my nose.

He frowned. "What's up, man?"

I blinked hard, pretending to find the right words. "What are your intentions with my sister?"

He glanced down the hallway, both sides, making sure no one was around. "Maybe you should come inside." He turned around and started to walk away from me. "I'm going, to be honest, I didn't take you for the brotherly type."

"I'm not," I replied, somberly.

"What-" He didn't get the chance to finish his sentence. I crushed the bottle against the back of his neck.

"Shit," Liam shouted, grabbing at the back of his neck.

"*Lévï Léah*," I whispered the spell easily. It had been my favorite since I got my magi. The force of my magic hit him square in the back. He fell to his knees and lifted his eyes to me. They were full of hatred. "*Morí Torrillé.*" His arms snapped behind his back. I moved my hand and released the spell that held his tongue to keep him from doing magic until the serum set in.

"Your father is going to have your neck." Liam seethed.

"How is he going to find out?" I crouched down in front of him.

He replied robotically. "I'm going to tell him."

"Not if I bind you to oath," I smirked.

I was surprised when he asked me another question passionately, trying to break through the serum. "How did you get the ingredients. Truth and oath potions are reserved for council members and the High Priestess." His eyes grew wide. "You found her?"

"Council members have ways of discovering things." I chuckled. "They break the rules too."

I checked my Magi. I was running out of time.

"Were you involved in Freya's disappearance?" I asked, keeping my anger in check.

Robotic. "No."

"Do you know who was?"

"Yes."

"I want names and reasons." I clenched my jaw.

"I don't have their names. They work anonymously." He gulped, the sound echoing in the room.

"So, someone hired them to kidnap Freya?"

Another gulp. "Yes."

"And who was that?" I almost enjoyed tormenting him by dragging it out.

"I don't know his name. It was someone in another coven. He's visiting."

"Does my father know he's here?" I asked.

"Probably not. I don't think he's staying here,

he's just aiding some witches." Liam gave me a scared look. "He's not someone you want to familiarize yourself with."

I narrowed my eyes at him. We only had a few minutes left of the truth serum. "Did you ask for his help? Did you call for him?"

"No. He said he is paying a friend a visit and tying up loose ends." He looked around the room as if we weren't alone. "He's scary. I'll admit, I don't want Freya as the High Priestess, but I wouldn't do anything to harm her. I'll protest the ancestors if I have to. But sacrificial magic? Never."

"You knew someone wanted to harm her though and you did nothing about it?" I crossed my arms over my chest to keep myself from killing him.

"What was I supposed to do? Defy this monster and possibly die?"

We got one monster out, just to get a new one in. "Where's Shay?"

He fought this question hard. Sweat started to bead on his forehead "She is from his coven, they came here together."

I picked up the lamp, and I ran it into the wall. I was an idiot. There had been too many coincidences lately, and I had been blind to the biggest one.

I pulled my Magi out and checked the time. We were out of it.

"I know what you have to do. I've never dealt with an oath potion before." Liam paused. "Will it hurt?"

"No," I crushed the bottle in my hand and blew the powder into Liam's face. "You won't speak of what happened in here, this is between us. If someone asks, you tell them I came to speak about your intentions for Ayre. You'll die before you speak of this. Magic will not work on you."

"So this shall be, my oath kept for thee." The words were almost sung by Liam, and he looked to be in a trance.

From what I had studied, everything was complete. I cleared the air of my spell and shook hands with Liam. He gave me a tight-lipped smile.

"I really do like Ayre," he said.

"Good, she really likes you. Don't screw this up." I winked at him.

When I pulled the door open, I came face to Face with Shay, her fist raised getting ready to knock.

Her mouth dropped open, and her eyes flicked between Liam and me. "Is everything okay here?"

She gave Liam a wide-eyed look. Like a deer caught in the headlights.

I laughed easily. "Why wouldn't it be?"

Her shoulders started to relax when Liam played right into my facade. "I don't think we have been properly introduced. Do you have the wrong room?"

Shay wiped her hands on her jeans. Her laugh wasn't as convincing. "No, I was looking for Sterling. His sister said I could find him here."

"That conniving little-" I acted angry, clenching my fist at my side.

She touched my arm and looked worried. "Please don't mention it. I want to earn her trust, and if she knows I told you, she'll be upset!"

I unclenched my fist. "Fine," I muttered. When I looked at Liam, he had his eyebrows raised. "We aren't done. Like I said, my sister is a lot of things, but she's my sister. If you hurt her, you'll have to find another coven."

Liam rolled his eyes and closed the door. Shay gripped my hand tightly, "What was that all about?"

"He likes my sister, and I wanted to make sure his intentions were pure." I shrugged.

"You sound like my father." She snickered and

shook her head. "That's how he was, at every turn. He would probably have your head if he knew where I was."

I frowned, still playing my part. "Why doesn't he know where you are?"

"My father had a lot to do with me having to flee Paris. I got into the wrong crowd, and I knew I had to leave to escape when I went to ask my father for help... he told me that I was an adult now and I had made my bed, I now needed to lie in it."

"Sounds a lot like my father." I bit into my cheek, wondering if there was truth in her words.

"Your father is a bit more level-headed than mine." She said solemnly.

"I'm really sorry about that. My father and I have our issues, but we can coexist. I'm sorry that you and your father can't."

CHAPTER SEVEN

FREYA

My strength had returned for the most part, but I still hadn't learned much about where I was. The sun was starting to peek through the windows, and I knew I needed rest, but I couldn't let myself. I needed to find a way out of here. The door opened, and Agata came in.

"I'm not bringing you clothes." It was the first thing she had said to me since I had wrapped my hands around her neck. "Whoever did this to you... Your coven needs to see this. They need to see what you went through in the bayou."

She was right. They needed to see what they were fighting for. The people that had done this to me were monsters. I nodded my head.

"I know the truth serum wasn't what you wanted or expected, but I would like to aid your coven when the time comes. My people are your people. We care about your coven and the Master's."

"Then why did you want to know what Sterling meant to me?" I pushed myself off of the dusty floor and leaned against the door.

"Because my daughter likes him." She smirked. "No ulterior motives there. She has worked with your coven in the past with Katrina efforts, and your coven helped us rebuild our pack during that time too."

I leaned against the wall and spoke, "What does this mean? Am I free to go?"

"Of course. You aren't a prisoner here. In fact, there is someone here that is very eager to see you." Agata smiled and opened the door. I limped toward the door, and when I made it there, I had to squint against the sun. People were crowded around the opening to the building, watching me with curious eyes. Some of the mothers covered their children eyes, while the others wanted their children to see the horrors of the world. I straightened my back and walked down the steps. We were on a raised building in the heart of the bayou. Raised structures weren't an uncommon sight around these parts. It flooded too often for the buildings to be on the ground. There was a worn dirt road that led to several other buildings just like this.

I was in the middle of a small community. I had no idea just how far from civilization I was. All of the people standing around me were different races. The majority of the people had beautiful ebony skin that matched Agata, but they all had bright crystal blue eyes.

What magical race had I stumbled upon?

"Welcome to The Hebert pack. My people haven't stopped speaking about you since you arrived." She bowed her head to me. "I welcome to you all the High Priestess of the New Orleans coven."

I whipped my head around and gave her a horrified look. I was no such thing, right? Sariah, my mother, had taken that position back when she had gone back to New Orleans from the Mirror Realm. Did this mean she was gone from our city? From the town, I had grown to love so much and miss terribly when I was away? How did this woman even know?

"From me, silly." A deep, sensual voice filled my mind, and nothing else mattered.

Strength flooded my body, and I flew down the steps. I searched frantically while I ran down the road, my heart pounding with each step. I knew I was getting closer and when I broke through the tree line.

There he was. My chest heaved, and I could barely feel the tears rolling down my face. My toes dug into the mud and pushed me faster as I raced for my red dragon. I struck him and threw my arms around his massive neck. His warm breath tickled my hair as chuckled in my mind.

"You're okay. You're okay." I chanted over and over as I rubbed my palm down his shining hard scales.

"*You're worried about me? You're the silliest human I have ever met. Have you seen yourself?*" he purred in my head.

"I can only imagine," I whispered.

"*Do you know what happened? If Agata hadn't mind shared with me, I probably would have burned her entire village down.*"

"You're the big bad wolf now?" I laughed. The sound was so foreign. "What do you mean mindshare?"

"*She has a special magic that allows her to share her body with a wolf. I think humans call them werewolves. This makes it easy for me to share information and not burn down villages."* I just hugged him tighter. *"I want to know what happened, but first I need to know you're okay."*

I just nodded and pressed my forehead against his massive body. Fatigue was finally starting to pull at my mind. "I'm okay, just sleepy." I removed the sheet around my body, and he extended his wing. I climbed up and onto his back like I had done when we were in the Mirror Realm.

"Rest, Freya. We will leave when night falls." Vailen whispered in my mind as I faded from consciousness.

VAILEN LANDED hard and jerked me from my slumber. It was a cloudy night in New Orleans, no stars could be seen. I could hear commotion happening on the ground but decided to remain hidden. I didn't want to be a part of it just yet. I buried my face in my familiar's scales and traced my finger over a horn jutting out of his back.

"Where have you been? It's been a week!" A familiar voice shouted from the ground. Vailen started to growl, and I could hear people shouting to move back. "Vailen, I'm serious. I was worried about you."

"It's almost your time to shine, lover boy is getting mushy on me."

I chuckled at that and sat up. There was a breeze in the air which meant it was the end of October. New Orleans could never make up its mind when it came to the weather. But cold weather didn't come around until about Halloween time. Vailen extended his wing and slowly shrunk down until he was about the size of a horse. I was now fully visible, and butterflies ignited in my stomach when my eyes landed on Sterling Masters. His hair was messy like it hadn't been trimmed since I left and there were patches of stubble sprouting out on his chin in random spots.

His mouth fell open slightly, and he gaped like a fish. "Freya." His voice was so tender it almost erased the date night from my mind. Almost. When I slid from Vailen's back, horror filled his face. I cringed as my bare feet touched the cold cobblestones. He took a step back and shook his head, horror eminent on his face. "What did they do to you?"

I knew there were others around, but all I could see was Sterling. Pain replaced the horror, and he fell to his knees in front of me. "I didn't realize I looked that bad."

"You look like you died." Ayre was the next one to come forward, her eyes looking over my body, as tears streamed down her face.

"I might have," I said.

"There is nothing to see here." Jonathan Masters came forward and wrapped his coat around me. His hands rubbed down my arms like he was trying to keep me warm. I couldn't feel a thing, except the stones I was standing on.

There were a few mutters of disapproval, but everyone left, dragging their feet as they went.

"We can't do this out here. Based on the marks on your body, you're lucky to be alive." Jonathan pulled Sterling from the ground and looked him in the eyes. "Get it together, that's an expensive suit, you could put holes in the knees."

Sterling yanked his arm out of his father's grasp and scowled. "Then I will pay to have it tailored. You would have reacted the same if you had seen mom like- like this."

Jonathan stopped and wrinkled his eyebrows. I was still too weak to make sense out of his words, but based on how Ayre and his father were reacting, they were big words.

When we got to Jonathan's study, he snapped his fingers, and the fireplace roared to life. He grabbed a blanket from the settee in the corner. He tossed it to Sterling and sat at his desk. He rested his face on his hands, and his eyes followed Vailen as he lazily entered the room.

"What happened?" Jonathan asked.

"Do we really need to do this right now? She looks like she needs to see a healer and rest!" Sterling argued.

"I'm fine." I held my hand up. I could speak for myself. I wasn't an injured animal. I had been to hell and back, but that didn't mean that I couldn't take care of my own. "I don't remember what happened. The last thing I remember was watching Sterling get into an argument with a woman and someone knocking me unconscious." I must have said the wrong thing because Jonathan gave his son a look that said they had something to discuss.

"What happened after that?" Ayre asked this time, much a much softer voice than what her father had started with.

"I woke up in the swamp. I had been underwater, struggling and then somehow I was flying from the muck and running from an alligator." They all looked at me shocked.

"Do you think you were in the swamp this entire time?" Sterling wrinkled his eyebrows and rubbed Vailen's back absentmindedly. Vailen was thumping his tail and purring, so that was a good sign.

"I don't know how I survived a few days in a swamp." I chuckled.

No one else laughed with me. "It's been a lot longer than a few days," Sterling said, gently.

"What?" The serious faces around me scared me. "How long?"

"It's the end of November."

Time lost. I had been so worried about it when I was with The Hebert Pack, but I had lost a lot more than I could have ever imagined.

I closed my eyes and felt the first wave of tears coming my way. I bowed my head. I was no longer okay. "I'm ready to go rest now." My voice sounded just as broken as I felt.

No one said anything as Sterling helped me stand. Vailen was quick on our heels. He was warming up to Sterling, but I doubted that he would let me out of his sight for a long time.

"*You are correct.*" I rolled my eyes. Leave it to Vailen to be listening to my thoughts, waiting for the right moment to butt in.

When we pushed my bedroom doors open, I took a step out to make sure I was in the right place.

I had been fighting back tears that I was afraid I had gone into the wrong room, or rather lead me into the wrong room on purpose. But sure enough, this was my room with Sterling's furniture.

"You aren't moving in here. Don't get the wrong idea." I said, grouchily.

He laughed. The sound making me want to throw myself at him and bask in his comfort. I held myself back. "I figured you might like it. I know you had other things picked out, but Ayre told me that they weren't your favorite and I thought maybe this would help you feel at home. It also kept me busy and gave me hope that you would come back."

My heart skipped a beat, I swear. I gulped and felt relief. It washed over me, but I held back the tears some more until I could get into the bathroom. But when I looked in the mirror... I lost it. There were handprints on my neck and bruising covering the rest of my pale skin. I could see almost all of my veins and where I couldn't, there was mud on me. Cuts and scrapes covered the other areas of my body, and I couldn't believe what I was seeing.

What happened to me?

Almost robotically, I removed what was left of my dress, which wasn't much, and my underwear. I threw it into the small garbage can under the sink and turned on the shower. When I stepped under the flow of water, it felt so good my spirit almost left my body. Probably not the best thought, especially after seeing the handprints on my body, but I had to find light somewhere.

When I was finished, there was a stack of clothes on the sink and two towels. I wrapped my hair up first then my body, I didn't have the energy for the pajamas. I dragged my feet and made it out of the bathroom. There were two chairs in front of the windows, and a sleeping Sterling had taken one of them hostage. Vailen was curled up on the bed sleeping just as soundly as the man across the room. I dragged myself back into the bathroom and donned the PJs before slipping under the covers.

CHAPTER EIGHT

STERLING

I didn't know what had woken me up, but I was glad it had. Freya was sound asleep, and the sun was shining through the lace curtains just enough to illuminate her red hair spanned out on the pillow beside her. She looked like magic. Vailen grumbled at me, almost as if he was telling me not to get any ideas. I held my hands up in surrender and then stretched. I could see the bruises on the fiery redhead still, and it made me insane with grief.

I scrubbed my hands down my face and winced at the stubble there. I needed to freshen up, but I knew it could wait. I preferred to stay here and watch Freya sleep. Vailen rolled his big green eyes, and all I could do was grin. I knew he was just as happy as I was that she was back. He had no reason to complain. Though he acted like an old man, so I was sure that had something to do with it.

The old coot.

Smoke started to curl from his nose, and I almost laughed at the threat he was insinuating. A soft yawn took my attention away from the monster in front of me. Freya squinted then frowned before she pushed herself up in bed. The purple and blue bruising around her neck had started to fade, but it was still very much there.

Freya wrinkled her nose at me and shook her head before she rubbed her eyes and looked at me again. "What are you doing here?"

I thought on my words carefully before I opened my mouth to speak. "I wanted to wait up for you last night. I tried my hardest to stay awake and honestly since you disappeared... last night was the first night I had actually slept."

She stared at me then looked at Vailen. Vailen must have been speaking to her because she was focusing intently on him. Her face softened when she looked back at me. "You went through all lengths to bring me back."

"Of course." I paused. I knew I was going to take this conversation in left field, but I knew I needed to get something off of my chest. "That night…"

She winced and looked away. She pulled the blanket up higher on her chest and rested her face on her bent knees. "You really don't have to do this, Sterling."

"But I do." I swallowed. "That night, it was all planned by someone to distract me so you would leave. It worked. Their entire plan almost worked."

She raised her head. "What?"

I began to explain what had happened after she had left and the confusion on the girl's face. How she didn't even know who I was or what was going. I closed my mouth and knew I need to put up a spell. "Hold on."

I stood up and spread my hands wide, I took a deep breath and walked to the door. I blew against the door, and blue fire rained down the wall. I did the same thing to the windows and the closet door. Freya stared at me with wide eyes and her mouth hanging open. "I have to make sure we don't have any unwanted visitors lurking about."

"This whole magic thing gets cooler and cooler every day," she muttered.

"Speaking of magic… I would imagine that Vailen told the pack of who you are." I said, slowly.

She nodded her head and scooted to the edge of the bed. She shook her head gently, and her red hair lifted from her shoulders. "Sariah is gone?"

"Somewhat." I tilted my head from side to side, trying to find the right words. "Vailen ran her out of the city, and she popped in to check on the coven briefly. She wanted to speak with you about something. She said you must be prepared for what is to come."

"What is that supposed to mean? What is coming?" She walked around the bed and put her hand on Vailen's head, almost like she was getting comfort from touching him. Her eyes got big as she remembered something and Vailen shot off of the bed. Smoke pumped from Vailen's mouth and nose, and he started to grow. Freya put her hands out and said, "Stop, it's okay. I'm not in danger anymore."

"What did you remember?"

"I know what's coming." All I could do was look at Vailen as she spoke. He closed his eyes and wrapped his wing around the front of his body.

"Well, don't leave me in suspense." I snapped.

"Rougarou." With that one word, I knew why Vailen was hiding.

"Is that what did this to you?"

She told me about what happened in the swamp, and I had to sit down. I couldn't believe what I was hearing. It had been hundreds of years since the Rougarou had taken over the swamp.

"Do you know what they are?" I asked her.

She shook her head. "I only know the stories. I thought it was the Cajun legend for werewolves."

"Kind of. A rougarou is a werewolf, one that has been twisted by dark magic."

I remembered the way Sariah had looked when she had popped in for a visit. There was no coincidence on the timeline. There couldn't be. A dark witch and now dark wolves popping up?

"Who do you think did this?" She asked the question, but her eyes held the truth. She knew who had done this.

Vailen got up then and pushed through my magical binds like they were water. He left a smoke trail behind him. "He didn't mess them up, did he?"

I shook my head and quickly walked to her side. "Look about what happened that night. That's not how I would have ended things. I enjoyed my time with you."

Her face was a portrait of hope as she looked up at me. Then she closed her eyes and turned away. I grabbed her hand and tried to pull her back to me. "I know about Shay."

One more roadblock in my way.

"Nothing has remotely happened with Shay."

"Vailen told me that you kissed her," she replied, cheeky.

"Vailen is a sneaky bastard and doesn't know when to leave things alone." I raised my eyebrows at her.

"What's going on?" she asked as I cupped her face in my hands.

"Shay is apart of the rebellion here. Everything that happens with her and I isn't real. I need you to know that first and foremost." My thumbs traced lazy circles on her cheeks. "Do you really think Vailen would be gone if he thought my feelings weren't true?"

"He did say that you have confided in him a lot lately."

I leaned in close, but the bruising on her hands and neck had me pulling away. She wrinkled her eyebrows at me and tried to see my face better. "What is it?"

The words wouldn't come out of my mouth. "I think you died." I choked on the words. "I don't know what brought you back, but these marks are deep. When we saw you last night, we knew this wasn't just somewhere they dumped you to die. They dumped you there so your body wouldn't be found."

Her face fell, and she stumbled backward as she tried to find something to hold herself steady. "How am I alive? How am I not hungry or thirsty or anything? How am I surviving on little to no food for weeks?" I could barely hear her as she whispered to herself.

When she looked up at me, her green reptilian eyes were full of tears. I cupped her face again before I pulled her to me. "I think it has to do with you being the High Priestess. It's what's kept you alive. When I was at the academy, I read a lot of books about the powers of the High Priestess, I wanted to understand my mother better. There are many things about being a High Priestess that haven't been uncovered yet, there is no telling, to be honest."

She nodded her head, trying to process it all.

"Are you hungry?" I asked.

She laughed. "I could eat an entire kitchen."

"With Shay, it's all pretend, you must remember that. Until I can get to the bottom of this." I took her hand in mine and squeezed it reassuringly before I let her go. I snapped my fingers, and the wards fell.

She gave me a snarky look and took off running. "Last one there is a rotten egg!"

I smiled as I let her get a good head start before I took off behind her.

CHAPTER NINE

FREYA

I was out of breath when I made it to the kitchen, Sterling was right behind me. Even though he had given me a tremendous start, he had caught up with me quickly.

"You're incredible, you know that right?" he asked, but it seemed more like a statement.

I made a face at him and shook my head.

Ayre was on our heels. She gave us looks and pulled the fridge door open. "Okay, Princess, what will it be?"

I tried to think of anything I had craved, but nothing came to mind. "Pancakes?"

She gave me an evil grin. "Perfect!"

When Ayre was finished, she set a plate of fluffy circles in front of me. She set down a jar of peanut butter and a bottle of syrup, "pick your poison."

I dumped a healthy amount of sickly sweet goodness on my carbs and dug in. Sterling looked at me with disappointment.

I stopped mid-chew. "Wfat?"

"Peanut butter is way better on pancakes," he said.

I rolled my eyes, laughed and continued to eat the deliciousness in front of me. It was nice to be back, but it felt strange. It felt odd to be normal and to have mundane interactions with each other.

"I hate to kill the mood..." Ayre started. I swallowed another mouthful and set my fork down. "But you need to go see a healer."

"I'm okay, really," I said.

"I know, but you were... gone... a long time and I'm worried about you." she finished.

I looked away from my friend and let my gaze settle on Sterling. He cocked his head and nodded. It was decided then, in order for things to go back to normal, I needed to be checked out.

I finished off the pancakes and went to wash my dishes. Ayre laughed and pushed me away from the sink. "Things are about to change around here."

Sterling grabbed my hand before she could

explain. He pulled me from the kitchen and down the hall.

"What did she mean?" I pulled my hand out of his.

"The High Priestess has too much to worry about to do dishes." I almost thought he was joking, then I saw his face.

"I'm not royalty. I haven't been here long enough to just put those things onto others." I stopped. "I'll never be here long enough to do that."

"It's just how it is. Don't insult your coven by not accepting it." He set his mouth into a hard line

THE HEALER WAS A TINY THING. Her mahogany hair fell past her butt, and she had a cute little hoop through her nostril. I could faintly see tattoos peeking out from the sleeves on her scrubs as she waved her hands around my body. A cloud of soft gold dust floated in the air around my body. She leaned forward to infect each spec. When she was finished, she took a seat next to the computer against the wall and shook her head.

"You are an anomaly." She leaned back and held her hand up. She moved her fingers toward herself in a come-hither motion, and all the gold flew right to her. She pinched the air in front of her pretty much zoomed in. The spec of dusk grew before our eyes. Sterling sat in the chair next to the table and looked at me like this was nothing.

As the dust got bigger, I realized that it wasn't dust at all. It was little images of my body. She zoomed out with her fingers, and the dust disappeared. She scratched her face. "Would you like Sterling to step out of the room?"

I nodded my head, I had no idea what she was about to lay on me. Sterling ducked out of the small room, but before he closed the door, he said, "I'll be right here. I'm not going anywhere."

I focused my attention on the healer. "You died."

Chills erupted all over my body. "I'm sorry?"

"I can see the pattern of decomposition that had happened in your body. It seems like your magic is healing you though. Regenerating cells and such." she said it like it was no big deal.

"Okay, that's normal then?" I asked.

Her lavender eyes got wide, and she scratched her face. "Oh, essence, no. This is very much abnormal. You should be dead."

"What does this mean for my future? For me? My magic?" The room spun around me.

"Have you noticed your magi lately?" She pointed at my wrist.

I had barely acknowledged it lately and hadn't even thought to check it after the truth serum. I looked down at it shocked. The colors had all changed on it, and I didn't know how I hadn't realized it sooner. The gems had gone from a deep red to a deep forest green.

"It almost matches your eyes." She gave me a reassuring smile.

"What does this mean?"

"There are many changes that you will experience with your magic and yourself over the next few weeks. That is the first sign that your magi and your mind have accepted the responsibility and role of being the High Priestess to our coven. All magis change when a new Priestess is called. I'm not sure why yours chose green." She got up and opened the door. "In a few weeks, I'm sure the bruising will be completely gone. It might take a little while because of the cell regrowth. In a few weeks, come see me, and I'll check you out again."

I nodded my head and mindlessly left the healer's quarters. Sterling followed behind me silently.

When we made it to his father's study, he stopped me. "You should know something."

I picked my head up. "What's that?"

"In the next few months, this will be your compound, and it will change accordingly. You will have responsibilities that my mother will prepare you for. This will no longer be my father's study. It will be yours."

Just another thing to stun me into silence. How did you even reply to something like that?

"Oh, okay." I walked through the open door. Camey was sitting at the desk, pouring over a book. She briefly looked up then back down.

"I see your magi changed," Camey said.

I knew she wasn't looking at me, but I shrugged. I was in an overwhelmed state, might as well just get everything over with at this point.

"What did the healer say?" Camey finally looked up from her book. Her hair was in her face, and she pushed it back and leaned forward.

I sighed. "I died."

Something crashed on the floor behind me. I slowly turned around. Sterling was picking up a metal vase off of the floor and set it back on its podium. I didn't mean to surprise him, but what other way was I supposed to say it?

Camey frowned. "I was worried that was what happened. Did she have any ideas on what saved you?"

"My magic. She said its regenerating cells at a rapid rate."

Camey's frown lifted, and she cocked her head. "There are many things make a High Priestess what she is. One of them is her power in her bloodline, on her mother's side. The other is how hard it is to kill one. For a while, I wondered if that was why your mother came back to the heart of New Orleans."

"So, it doesn't matter if you are good or bad, you're a High Priestess by birth?" I asked.

"Kinda," She paused. "When you and your mother were gone, the torch was passed to me, temporarily because of my bloodline. My mother's side has been serving the High Priestesses in New Orleans for hundreds of years. I may be a little ditzy and air-headed, but I know my role."

I twisted my fingers in front of me. "What's going to happen to me?"

"You will find that your magic has a stronger hold on you. The first sign will be the change in color of your magi. You will have a lust for magic, it will itch under your skin, and you will have to release it. Some of your senses will heighten, and you won't need a spell, incantation or serum to do what you need to." she said.

"Does that include truth serums?" The words made me cringe. I didn't know if I would ever be able to perform that on another person.

"Yes, but usually it is the coven's council member that does that. Unfortunately, you can't do it all. You will burn yourself out." She folded her arms in front of her chest. "I tried, I tried to do it all, and all it did was make my brain cells disappear at a faster rate," she laughed. "and make me lose touch with my family."

Sterling looked away and pretended to be browsing the shelves for a book.

"I guess, I just need to know what this means for me." I looked at the worn rug under my feet.

"Well, you haven't been openly accepted by our coven, but hopefully that will turn around soon. Ayre has some plans with a certain witch." She pushed away from the desk and stood up, but before she came in my direction, she grabbed a stack of papers off of the desk. She handed them to me and smiled. "We can't introduce a new High Priestess without a proper celebration."

The invitations were beautiful, they were white

with gold calligraphy. The formal party would be in two weeks. I looked up at Camey's beaming face. She was so proud of what she had put together.

"I'll be properly introduced to the coven this night?" I asked, just making sure. I would need to mentally prepare myself.

"Yes! It will be a huge celebration." She left me with one invitation and took the rest back to the desk. She leaned against the desk and looked at Sterling. "You can go now."

He didn't say anything and left.

"You know, you can take Sterling with you. He is determined to not leave your side, and it would give y'all an excuse to redo the date." She lifted her eyebrows suggestively.

I laughed and whipped my head around, making sure that he was nowhere near the study. "I don't know about that."

"Sterling is a lot of things, but he has changed. I didn't think it would happen in such a short amount of time, but he realized what is important and what isn't now. You helped him see the light." She chuckled and took a seat behind the desk. "Pretty soon this will be your space, and I can't wait for the day."

CHAPTER TEN

STERLING

I leaned against the wall and waited for Freya to come out of the study. I knew better than to try to eavesdrop on their conversation. My mother had the room spelled like no one's business. She liked the study for that reason. It was the one place in the entire compound that was considered a 'safe zone.' I could hear footsteps coming from down the hall, and I straightened, not really ready to talk to someone, especially if Freya came out soon.

My worst fear became a reality as Shay rounded the corner. She was holding a white piece of paper in her hand with a huge smile on her face. "Hey, you!"

I tried my best to smile back. "Hey, you." I sucked at flirting, especially when it was forced.

"Did you see?" She laughed and rolled her eyes. "Never mind, of course, you did your mother is the one in charge!"

I tried my hardest not to let my horror show on my face. *The party.*

"I know this isn't how it goes and I am probably stepping out of line here, but I have had so much fun with you since being here, that I wouldn't dare think of bringing anyone else." She twisted a dark strand of hair around her finger and gave me a coy look. "So, would you do me the honors of being my date?"

Exactly what I was afraid of.

"Yes." The word came out before I even knew what was happening.

She threw her arms around my throat and pulled my face down to hers and kissed me. I was only partially there because as soon as our lips met, I heard Freya leaving the study and Shay had me in a death lock. When she finally let me up for air, Freya was gone.

"I haven't seen much of you today, where have you been hiding?" Shay asked.

I looked at the direction that Freya had disappeared to before giving my attention back to Shay. "Freya came back last night."

Shay pouted. "Oh."

"Yeah, she was pretty rough. I fell asleep in her room making sure she was okay and comfortable." I cleared my throat, feeling even more uncomfortable.

She clucked her tongue. "Your sister couldn't have done that?"

I shrugged. "I don't know, I was worried about her."

She nodded her head and looked away from me. I had definitely said the wrong thing. "Well, I guess I need to find a dress for the party. I thought your mother was just being presumptuous. I didn't realize that Freya was back already. She had everyone so worried, for what? Just for her to turn around and come home." She rolled her eyes.

"She died," I said a matter of fact.

She blanched at that, and her eyes got big. "Maybe I should just shut my big mouth."

"That would be wise." I shook my head and walked away, determined to see where Freya had escaped to.

AYRE HAD FOUND me wondering the compound in search of Freya. I knew we hadn't established romantic feelings or even had a proper date since what had happened, but she had just witnessed me locking lips with the enemy. I had told her that is was all pretend, but seeing it in person couldn't be easy. Especially if she did have feelings for me. Which I hoped.

"Why do you look like a kicked puppy?" Ayre asked, as she scooped up a big heaping of jambalaya and shoveled it into her mouth. It smelled delicious, but I was too worried to eat. I could hardly eat anything lately.

"Shay asked me to the party," I said, trying to keep my voice light in case anyone was listening.

Ayre wrinkled her nose in disgust. "Yuck, and you said yes?"

I laughed, "Yes, I like Shay."

"I really can't understand why." She knew I was pretending, but she definitely wasn't. She was open about a lot of things, especially how she felt about most people.

"Don't be ugly," I said. "Have you seen Freya?"

She gave me a look that said she had finally caught on to why I looked so distraught. A very suggestive look that turned her entire face into an iPhone emoji. "Yes, she was learning how to cloak herself in the study with mom, and she wanted to test it out on Vailen and see if they could get some air." She laughed. "Literally."

"Flying around the city? That's a new one for sure." I frowned.

"What is it?" Ayre asked, sensing that there was more.

"Freya saw me kissing Shay."

Ayre inhaled right as she was taking a bite and started to cough uncontrollably. She breathed in the damn rice. She bent over and slapped her exposed leg as she continued to hack. After letting her die a little, I said, "*Avai*," and her throat cleared. It was the perfect spell.

"Waited long enough." She scowled at me and picked her jambalaya up off of the concrete by her feet.

"Eh, you needed to suffer a little bit." I laughed and slapped her on the back. Her very bareback. I took a step back and looked her up and down. "Do you want to explain to me why you are so exposed today? It's chilly, and you're showing leg and arms... and back..." I trailed off, suspicious. Her whole face lit up with pink. She turned away from me and started to walk away. "You need a sweater.

If dad saw you, he would have to kill many of the witches around here."

She rolled her eyes and turned around to keep walking away. "Men are always too dramatic. Who says that I need a reason to dress a certain way? Maybe I do this for myself because it makes me feel good."

I gave her a look that I wasn't buying it. "Where's Liam?"

She went pink again. "Shut up."

"I'm serious." I bumped my shoulder into hers and made her hit a pillar head-on. Her jambalaya hit the floor and rice went flying everywhere. When she turned around, I was already running. "Should have just been honest. The essence loves her karma!"

My good mood from being with my sister, instantly went into a bad mood as I turned a corner and hit my father head-on. It was the middle of the day, he should have been in the office. What was he doing here so early?

He gave me a severe look. "Someone let Freya leave the compound on the back of a dragon in broad daylight."

I wanted to laugh because this just added to Ayre's karma. Oh man, and if father saw her now. I pointed in the direction of my sister. She was wailing about how disrespectful I was and how rude and blah blah. "The culprit is on her way to us now."

I folded my arms over my chest and waited for it all to unfold. As soon as Father saw Ayre in her little outfit, all thought of Freya was gone, and I was forgiven.

"Do you want to explain to me what you are wearing?" *Here we go.*

Ayre looked down at herself casually. "This is called a romper, Father. Welcome to the 21st century, where women wear what makes them feel good."

Our father quirked an eyebrow inquisitively. "Oh, is this true?"

"Yes," Ayre gave me the look of victory.

"I would suggest that you stop gallivanting around in things that show off your entire body, but that is because you are my daughter and I don't appreciate viewing you in this manner." He paused and pinched the bridge of his nose. This was not going in the direction that I had hoped. Since when was Father progressive? "You're still my baby girl."

Ayre nodded her head and went in for a huge. Of course…

"You aren't off the hook for letting Freya leave on an extinct creature in the middle of the day in the heart of The French Quarter. Walk with me." My father tucked her hand into his elbow and lead her away from me. She would probably get away with it. She was the *baby* after all.

CHAPTER ELEVEN

FREYA

I closed my eyes and relaxed. I felt the pressure of the world fade away, and nothing else seemed to matter but being above the clouds.

High Priestess…

I snapped my eyes back open and jerked. Vailen felt me tense up, and he did the same. We started to drop a bit, but he recovered quickly.

"What is it?"

"I heard a voice," I said.

"I didn't hear anything." Which meant I was probably going crazy because if it was in my mind and he was bonded to me, wouldn't he hear it too?

High Priestess… it's time to go back to the place where this all started…

"Vailen, I think we need to land," I whispered, trying to hear the whispers in the air around me.

Vailen dipped low and did as I commanded.

Back to the horde of magis, Priestess…

Why would I need to go back there?

"Take me back to the compound. You're going to have to be really small for what's about to happen next."

Vailen snaked his head around and then dove. I was hopeful that our wards were still in place to keep us hidden, but if they weren't, I was too gone to worry about it. When we landed, I slid off of Vailen's back and marched to my room. Vailen followed me hesitantly. I pulled the backpack out from under my bed and considered bringing it to the little shop in the Quarter before I thought better of it.

What if Wyna wasn't on my side? What if this caused even more chaos? I shoved the backpack under the bed again and decided that it didn't matter. The Quarter was full of weirdos and oddities.

Vailen must have read my mind. He shrunk himself down and landed on my shoulder. He wrapped his tail around my neck like a piece of jewelry, and we were off. I could hear Jonathan shouting behind me as I went, but I paid no mind. I had a feeling that the ancestors had me on a mission and I was determined to find out why. I didn't know how I was going to find this shop, but I didn't have any other choice but to search.

"Did you lose your hearing up there?" Sterling jogged to catch up with me.

"Nope." I kept walking.

"You're ridiculous." He pulled me to a stop. "Where do you think you're going?"

"I need to find the shop with the magis," I said, almost robotically.

"I don't know why you didn't say that, to begin with." He rolled his eyes then noticed Vailen on my shoulder. "You're going to catch a lot of attention with that and your eyes."

I had completely forgotten about them. I touched my cheeks self consciously and started to worry.

"It's okay, Ayre is coming with some sunglasses now." He snatched them off of Ayre's face. She started to complain, but he was quick to explain. "We can't take any chances. The dragon is one thing, but the eyes too? We don't need any questions in the quarter. It isn't dark yet, or I wouldn't care. It's bad enough that Ayre and I have purple eyes."

You must hurry...

"I'm not worried with it. Just take me to the shop." I started to walk, and pretty soon Ayre was leading the way, but that didn't stop her from throwing strange looks over my shoulder. New Orleans was alive and well all around me. The smells of spices and the sounds of jazz wrapped around me, but I didn't let it distract me. The Quarter was a lively place unless it was the weekend and two am. I shook my head. I couldn't go there. The whispers had warned against distractions, and I was in the city made for them.

The souvenir shop was waiting for us like before. We went to the back of the store, and all Ayre had to do was touch the wall and it revealed itself. We stepped through the small doorway, and we were there. I didn't know what I was looking for, so I stayed still for a moment, letting the musty smells take over me.

The witch that had helped me before and had given Vailen's dragon egg came forward. Her face was bare of all emotion. She said nothing but watched us closely. Vailen was the first one to make a move. He rose off of my shoulder and started to sputter nonsense in my mind. Smoke was billowing from his nostrils. I followed his line of sight and sitting right above the doorframe, where his egg had been, was another. Except this one was white.

Do not delay...

I shook my head, trying to clear the whispers, but they just got louder and louder until I doubled over in pain. Vailen was in a frazzled state and hardly worried with my state of discomfort. Sterling pitched forward and grabbed me, keeping me from hitting the floor.

"What is it?" Ayre asked.

I shook off Sterling's hands. "The ancestors..." I paused. "They want the egg." At least I hoped it was the ancestors. It was just a theory at this point.

Ayre wrinkled her eyebrows. "There's another one?" She looked at the woman that owned the shop. "Madam Shriek, why didn't you tell us there was another?"

"I don't live in the compound, though I heard the rumors of the dragon, I didn't believe them." She said with perfect English. "It appeared this morning. Next to the magi boxes."

My head was still fuzzy, so I pointed to it and tried to grab Vailen. "Sterling, do you mind getting it down?" He was a good head taller than me, so it made sense.

Madam Shriek watched his every move. "I will get you something to put it in."

She disappeared, and Sterling held the thing like it was a deranged cat, out and in front of him. He watched it with careful, worried eyes. "What do I do with it?"

"I would imagine that Vailen would like to be next to it, so we'll see what Madam Shriek brings you," Ayre said.

I leaned against one of the shelves and watched Vailen slowly lower himself beside me. "What's wrong?"

"I shouldn't speak of such things. It could only bring death and destruction to us."

Lovely.

Madam Shriek came back holding two back-packs. One that matched the one Vailen had destroyed when we were in the Mirror Realm when he burst from the egg and another for Sterling. She handed them to us both before she turned to me.

"You are young, but you will do many great things. Don't let distractions pull you away from our ancestors and their influence." She bowed before she disappeared from the room.

"Why do I have this bad feeling in the pit of my stomach?" Ayre asked.

"Can we just get out of here?" Sterling asked second.

I tried to get Vailen to go into my backpack, but he wasn't letting the egg out of his sight.

Traitor.

I CLOSED MY BEDROOM DOOR, Vailen had abandoned me for his new fixation. I was just as curious as he was, but there was something more there. He was quiet inside my head, and I knew that he wouldn't be back anytime soon. I sat cross-legged on my bed and snapped my fingers. Flames licked up my fingers and danced in a teasing manner along my skin.

It wasn't hot or cold, it was just there like it was apart of me. I patted my hand to try to put it out, but it was no use, the flame parried up my arm and to my shoulder. The material of my clothes started to turn to ash before my eyes, and before I knew it, my entire body was engulfed. I jumped from the bed and turned in a circle. My body was entirely on fire, the only part that wasn't was my feet. I stared at my hands in horror and tried to calm it down. Tried to put it out, closed my eyes and tried to pull the energy back inside of me. Nothing worked.

My magi glowed mischievously under all the orange, and I wanted to scream. I knew I had to play this calmly and carefully though. I didn't need to alert anyone of what was happening. I needed to get all of this under wraps.

A light tap on the door had me panicked, and the flames just jumped higher. The tap happened again, but there was nothing I could do. How was I supposed to invite someone in like this? The knocking was becoming more frantic now. The door burst open and standing in the doorway was Sterling and Vailen. Sterling's face went from shock to lust to embarrassment. What was I supposed to do? There was no innocence when all the fire did was eat everything up.

Sterling looked at my face and then at the ceiling over and over before he just closed his eyes.

"*Relax, child.*" The sound of Vailen's voice took away most of my worries, and I felt my shoulders start to slump. "There is nothing to be afraid of."

I nodded my head.

"*Take a deep breath, I think I have an idea.*"

Vailen breathed in profoundly then blew out a frigid air onto me. It wrapped around me like a cold blanket, and the flames disappeared. I grabbed at the purple duvet on the bed and pulled what I could around my shoulders. There were a few singed holes in it, and I felt guilt eating at my insides. Sterling was staring at me again, but this time with a strange fascination.

He opened his mouth to speak, but I beat him to it. "I don't care what kind of act of Congress needs to take place in order for this to happen, but I want lessons. I want to know as much as I can. Why are these things happening to me? How do I control it? Why are there spells and potions, but yet, I can just burst into flame?"

When I stopped speaking, I was panting. Sterling's face softened and went to the chair he had fallen asleep in the night before. "No act of Congress." He chuckled. "I'll see what I can do. I will have to appeal to a council member."

"Lucky you, one is your father," I said.

"Eh, not so lucky, but a little easier." He shrugged, then winked.

CHAPTER TWELVE

STERLING

I paced the floor in the study. It felt strange to not call it his office anymore. I was sure I was also the culprit of the worn boards in this specific spot. It was my preferred waiting area for when my father had time and would try to fit me in.

"What is so urgent?" My father pushed the doors open behind me. He unbuttoned his suit coat before he took a seat behind the desk.

"Freya was on fire." I paused and considered my next few words carefully. "In her room, alone, panicking." I wanted to add in, completely nude, but I knew that would spark new lust within me and I didn't need to explore that at this moment. At the thought, I could feel heat filling my face.

My father quirked his brows and narrowed his eyes. "How did you know?"

"Vailen was with me."

"The beast left his familiar?" Father asked, concerned.

"Not for very long," I replied.

"What could be so important to drag him away?"

I ran my tongue over my teeth, thinking. "We found something at Madam Shriek's shop."

"You're going to make me ask?" He lifted his eyebrows.

"Another dragon egg," I whispered.

Father flew from his seat. "What do you mean?"

I didn't want it to get out. I knew father would be the best person to tell, but it made me nervous. "Lower your voice."

"Are you certain?" He looked at the door behind me.

"Yes, and Vailen will only let me handle it. I'm surprised that he isn't here now." I touched the backpack on my back with tenderness.

"That's why you have that silly thing, I was wondering." He muttered.

"But that's not why I'm here." I paused. "Freya

needs training. How is she supposed to protect us or do any of her duties? She can't control her magic."

"I was aware that she had been working with Vailen before she disappeared."

I shook my head. "This isn't something he can help her with."

He crossed his arms and leaned on the desk. "Very well. What do you suggest?"

"She needs to attend the institute," I said.

"She will not have the time to be there. In the coming weeks, she will have much to do. Grade school is the last place for a High Priestess." Father shook his head and rubbed a finger along the book-case next to him. "What does your schedule look like? Have you chosen what you want to do with your life?"

It was a depressing admittance that I hadn't. I shook my head. Why was this something that I needed to be worried about right now? Like I didn't have enough on my plate as it was.

"Perfect, then all of your free time is now Freya's." Father's mouth quirked up, amused. "You will teach her about our history, the monsters that we coexist with and help her harness the magic inside of her."

I went to object. I was trying to find out information on Shay and the man that had come to town with her. I didn't have time.

"If you can't do this assignment, I can find another young man." He scratched his head. "I have one in mind, he has a little crush, but I've been known to play matchmaker before."

Manipulative Bastard. A feeling started to unfold in my stomach, and I knew I couldn't back out. I was damn near jealous, and I had no right to be. I wanted more, but I was playing a dangerous game with Shay. "Fine."

A mischievous twinkle lit in father's eyes. "Just what I wanted to hear."

I left the office in deep thought. I didn't know how I could possibly make it work. I rounded the corner at the kitchen and come face to face with Shay. She had a slice of cold pizza in one hand and a water bottle in the other. She gave me a soft closed-lipped smile, her cheeks full of food and for a moment I forgot that she was suspect number one. I felt myself relax and I hated that she had that effect on me.

She swallowed and threw the rest of the pizza in the trash, then wiped her hands on her jeans. She rested her hand on my shoulder and frowned,

"What's the matter?"

I sighed. She might as well know. "My father has asked me to tutor Freya."

I expected jealousy, but instead her eyes lit up suspiciously. "You've been asked to tutor the High Priestess? What an honor! Have you accepted?"

"I'm not sure." I hesitated, playing a game with her. I wanted to know her reaction. It was important for some reason.

She gave me a breathtaking smile. "I think you should accept. You'll be able to earn her trust and isn't that important to you?"

I folded my arms over my chest and leaned against the cabinets. "But it'll take me away from you."

She smiled and rubbed her hands down my arms. "Its okay, I would love to be able to get closer to her too."She rubbed up against me, almost like a cat in heat.

"I was afraid of what you would say." I paused. "I didn't know how I felt about being asked of this."

"You'll do great, I have no doubt. And maybe, I'll make a new friend." Her shoulders slumped. "I have to admit something."

Curiosity took hold of me. I waited for her to continue on.

"I was a bit jealous of her. Especially when she

disappeared. I felt like she was all you care about, but now that I know it's just because she's the High Priestess... it makes it easier for me to accept her and like her." She looked down at her feet, embarrassed.

I didn't know if it was an act or she was really vulnerable. I brushed a strand of her hair behind her ear, my emotions causing me to do things I didn't want to. I didn't know if my tenderness was an act or not, and it was complicating matters.

She stood up on her tippy toes, and I watched as she leaned in closer. She closed her eyes, and her lips met mine. They were soft and full against mine.

"Barf." The sound of Ayre's voice had me jumping back. "I thought you had gotten rid of her and found someone better."

I shook my head at her and tried to pretend to be angry. I blinked my eyes hard. "Ayre, don't Start. This is not the time or the place."

I was surprised when Shay whipped around and pointed her finger at Ayre. "You will mind your tongue in my presence."

Ayre smirked. "Ohh, a finger. I'm so afraid."

Something sinister lit up in Shay's eyes and Ayre grabbed at her throat in panic. I watched in horror as my sister's feet left the ground and she was suspended mid-air above the island. Tears streamed down Ayre's face, and the only expression on Shay's face was cold hatred.

I touched Shay's arm, and Ayre crumpled to the floor. I rushed to her side but didn't take my eyes off Shay.

"You'll do best to remember that all witches are different. You'II do best to remember that your powers aren't matched with mine." Shay turned on her heel and disappeared from the room.

"You shouldn't have provoked her. We didn't know the extent of her powers, she could have killed you, then what?" I looked over her neck, checking for bruising. She winced and closed her eyes.

"I wasn't thinking," she whispered.

"You can't tell anyone about this. especially Father." I said, softly before I grabbed her hands and helped her stand.

"And why the hell not?" she shouted in my face.

I motioned for her to lower her voice. I didn't know if anyone was listening in or not. The act would have to continue on. "Because I like her and Father will have her sent away."

"Yes, because there is a strict rule on violence against your coven. It can be punishable by death."

She shook her head, her face bright with anger. "She is too powerful, I should have been able to see her magic. Something isn't right."

Then it clicked. Shay was the next High priestess for the Paris coven. It explained her magic. But we would have been able to recognize her last name.

Unless it was fake. My eyes got wide at my realization. Just when I was about to tell Ayre about my discovery screams echoed through the hallway. Ayre jerked forward and took off in a sprint. The look she gave me was pure terror, and I knew she was thinking the same thing.

Freya.

CHAPTER THIRTEEN

FREYA

I heard the screams from my room. I had been staring at the bag Wyna had given me. Wondering if it was safe to even touch. Vailen watched me with curious eyes but didn't say anything.

I jumped off the bed and tossed the bag under the bed. Vailen was out of the room faster than me. I about threw myself over the railing to see what the commotion was.

"*You will land on your feet, you have been gifted my reflexes,*" Vailen whispered in my mind.

A boy was being carted into the courtyard by a group of witches... Blood covered them all and I didn't think, I just jumped. I landed in a crouch. I felt eyes boring into me as I straightened up. When

I looked up, I was staring into Sterling's eyes. His face was a mask, and I desperately wanted to know what was going on in his turbulent mind. I could see it in his eyes, but that was where it stopped.

Vailen interrupted my musings. "*You are the High Priestess now, this is something you must take charge of.*"

I held my head high and marched to the crowd around the boy. He had been mauled by something, and my stomach dropped at the smell. The people parted as I got closer. Their eyes pleading with me.

"*What do I do?*" I thought to Vailen.

Silence was my answer. I was on my own.

The stench surrounding the small child was almost too much to bear. A woman held onto him for dear life. Everyone was quiet, but her. I had no doubt that she was his mother. Her dark skin was wet with tears. I touched her shoulder gently, and a jolt went through me. I was taken from the courtyard and floated above the Quarter.

The scene of what happened played out before my eyes. Just as I suspected. There was a rougarou in the heart of our city. I had almost forgotten about the one in the swamp, it made sense that it would follow me here. Just as quickly as I was taken from my body, I was put back. I took a deep breath and the whispers started around me.

"*You can heal the boy, but it will come with a price.*" The whispers circled me. "*A life for a life.*"

I noticed the mother's protruding belly, tears filled my eyes. The essence would take her unborn child. Who was I to make such a decision? Blood covered the boy from head to toe. He didn't even look like a person anymore. Slashes and cuts showed peaks of bone all over his body. I knew in my soul that it was much too late. I closed his eyes and shook my head. Deep within me, I knew this wouldn't be the last death.

Pain pierced through my being. I could hardly breathe as the words left my lips. I didn't even sound like myself. "There is nothing to be done. May the ancestors guide his spirit to rest."

His mother's wails followed me to my room and would haunt me till the day I left this world. The tears came swiftly and were unrelenting. When I finally fell to my bed, Vailen wrapped himself around me.

"*I will do what I must to protect you from the physical pain of the world; unfortunately, I can't do much to help with the spiritual.*" Vailen rumbled in my head. "*But I will do my hardest to stand by you and help you heal through it.*"

I ran my fingers down his snout and closed my

eyes. The tears had slowed down, but the pain was still there eating a hole in my soul.

"Can you hear the whispers?" I asked out loud, just as Sterling pushed the doors open.

Vailen shook his head against my leg. "*No, but I can feel them and know when they speak to you. We mind share. So when they are done, your thoughts give it all away.*"

Sterling fell to his knees in front of me and took my hands in his. The grief was written all over his face. "My father has called a Council meeting. They need to know what you saw."

"When?" My voice came out as a croak.

"Now."

I STARED at all the Council members surrounding me. They were mostly men except for one woman. She wore traditional African wear. An elaborate Caftan; around the neckline and sleeves, held intricate em bordered patterns. Her braided hair was kept away from her face with a matching scarf. Her deep brown eyes bore into mine.

"Repeat it again." Her words were thick with a British accent.

I closed my eyes and tried to keep my emotions

in check. The first time I had told them, I hadn't been able to keep it together. I took a deep breath.

"A rougarou was in the swamp where I was dumped, left for dead." I gulped, and corrected it, "where I was dead."

There was a commotion through the members. "Is there an investigation being conducted?"

Jonathan cleared his throat, and the room quieted down. "Yes, an investigation is happening. That isn't why we are here. There is someone with the power, creating these monsters. They are twisting these creatures into their minions. When was the last time we fought these?"

A man at the end of the room spoke. "It was over a hundred years ago. I would have to dig up the forbidden files."

I wanted to ask what the files were, but I kept my mouth closed. I didn't need them to think I was any more below them than they already believed. Or what I imagined they thought.

"You think someone is creating them, what if Sariah let them free when she escaped?" The African woman said.

"That's a possibility, but at this moment, we don't suspect her," Jonathan said. "She offered aide to our coven. She said we will need her for what is to come. She was afraid. I've never seen her afraid as long as I've known her and we all know that has been a long time."

Another man spoke up. He was wearing a tank top and ripped jeans with tattoos covering his arms. "And you haven't thought that maybe the baron lands changed her?" He rolled his eyes.

Jonathan said nothing and chose to ignore his comment.

"So, this beast was spotted in New Orleans?" The man at the end said.

"Yes," I muttered.

He thought for a moment and then spoke. "I propose we leave this to the New Orleans coven care."

"Aye." Everyone, but Jonathan, said in unison.

Before my eyes, everyone *poofed* away into a cloud of smoke. Jonathan sunk into the desk chair.

"What just happened?" I asked.

"We were overruled. They will not get involved."

"I bet they would if I told them I had a freakin' dragon," I muttered.

"We can't do that," Jonathan said, scrubbing his hands down his face.

"And why not?" I sunk to the floor, defeated.

"Because they would vote to take him from you. The Council is very..." He paused. "protective of the covens, but its their way or no way." In this moment, he reminded me of Sterling. "Which I won't let happen, but together, with all of The High Priestesses, their power is unmatched."

"So, what do I do?" I whispered, pulling at the threads on the rug. "Do we keep this a secret? Our coven already knows."

"We can't hide it, but we won't disclose it. They will not investigate based on the rumors, and by the time they do, your bond will be too strong." He raked his fingers through his neatly combed hair.

He stood up from the desk and came to me. I whispered as he helped me up. "What do I do?"

"Nothing just yet. You need to mourn your first loss." He stood next to me awkwardly. "I'm going to announce a curfew. I think the beast was after you. They can sense your magic. Other witches will get hurt with them coming for you."

I walked beside him out of my future office. "How do you kill a rougarou?"

"I don't know. " He shrugged. "Probably decapitate them. We will know soon enough once Leaf goes to the Forbidden Files."

It was my opportunity. "What is that place, besides the obvious?"

Jonathan waved his hands around, and red sparks made a field surrounding everywhere we walked. "We can talk frankly now. The Forbidden Files is common knowledge, but not where it is. The vault is in Europe and only the council, and High priestesses know where it is. Priestesses are only allowed to know by Council vote. You may never have that access unless its an emergency."

"My mother?" I asked as we got near the stairs that lead to my room.

"She was never voted clearance." He shook his head. "Its all blood and magic and of course, politics. Honestly, if she had been voted in, the wards wouldn't have let her in. They would have sensed the darkness inside of her."

My mind was spinning. There was just so much to this world, and I hadn't even breached the surface yet. I had to learn about The Mirror Realm, I had to get used to it, and I hadn't even learned about the world I came from.

Jonathan grasped my shoulder and gave it a gentle shake. "Get some rest. Have Sterling teach you to ward your room."

"Do you know where I can find him?" I asked.

All he did was point at my door, turned and walked away. I turned around, and he was leaning in my doorway.

"Oh," I whispered.

Sterling smirked. "He wants me to teach you wards to keep me out."

I tried to keep the laughter out of my voice. "Maybe."

"How are you feeling?" he asked.

I shrugged up one of my shoulders. "Kind of numb."

"What's the verdict?" He sat on the bed, next to Vailen, who was wrapped protectively around the sparkling dragon egg. He wasn't giving me any insight into what was going on in his mind either. I wondered if he only felt this way because he wanted to protect his dragon species.

I pulled myself from my thoughts. "There will be a curfew. We have to protect the coven. The rougarou is after me."

"What did the Council say?" he asked.

"We are on our own," I whispered. "A man named Leaf is going to help, but I think that's as far as it'll go."

Sterling nodded his head and absentmindedly petted Vailen. The beast rolled his eyes.

"He must think I'm a damned dog." Smoke rose from his nostrils. Sterling whipped his hand back quickly. "He'll learn."

"So, my father approved tutoring," Sterling said.

That perked me up quick. "Really?"

He nodded then shoved his hands into his suit pockets. The movement caused his button down to peak open, and I got a glimpse of his Magi.

He held his hand out to me, and I put my hand in his. "I'm your tutor." He shook my hand like we had never met before.

Butterflies ignited in my stomach. I wasn't sure if it was a good thing or a bad one that we would be spending more time together. "Great because I have like a million and one questions to get us started."

"Woah, there, killer." Sterling held his hands up and chuckled. "We are not starting tonight. It's too late."

Vailen rolled his eyes again.

"Fine, but you better be ready because I'm not going to slow down." I winked at him. "You better believe I won't be easy on you."

"Have you ever taken it easy on me?" He laughed.

"Nope and I don't plan on starting now!"

CHAPTER FOURTEEN

I ran my fingers down the spines of the books in the library. It wasn't anything special, but it housed knowledge like no other. There was something incredible about being in the place that Merlin once stood. This had been his private study when he came to visit his children, and I hoped that Freya asked about it all. It was, after all, the story of our people and how we came to be.

For a moment I wondered if I had chosen the wrong time to come here, the wrong time to teach Freya. All around me were students reading and catching up on assignments. I scratched my head and looked up from the books at just the right moment. Freya was tucking a loose strand of hair behind her ear while she approached me slowly. She had a notebook clutched tightly against her chest and was wearing jeans and a sweater. Vailen trailed lazily behind her, his tail dragging the ground with each step.

Freya looked down at him at the same moment he looked up to her, and I knew they were conversing. She rolled her eyes, and he stopped walking like he was throwing a tantrum. The look on both of their faces said it all.

Freya sighed and stopped. "You didn't bring the egg," she muttered like she hadn't wanted to bring it up.

"Yes, I did." I pointed to the table off to the side that had my pack slung over a chair. Vailen didn't look my way, but walked over to my chair, pulled the pack off and the curled his body around it. "Has he divulged any information?"

She shook her head, watching him sadly. "No, but I think it's because he's lonely. I think he's afraid of being the last of his kind."

I could see how that would be depressing. "Are you ready to get started?"

She shrugged up one of her shoulders. "About as ready as I'll ever be." She cleared her throat and asked the first question, "Why were dragons killed off?"

Oh, here we go. Starting off with the hard ones. "There are many things I don't know or understand about The Mirror Realm or its inhabitants, but I do remember the stories my father told when we were young." I paused and watched as she leaned over the table, getting closer to me as her eyebrows stretched to her hairline. "Dragons were always misunderstood. When they want to be, they can be monstrous and scary." I paused. "Help me out here, Vailen." My mouth went dry, and I didn't know why I was starting to feel so uncomfortable. Maybe because it wasn't my history to tell.

Freya jerked forward, and she let out a loud gasp. She blinked her eyes, and when they opened again, they were a deep green, entirely reptilian. *Hey, there, Vailen.*

A deep silky voice erupted from Freya's lips. "Witches were a weak link for many centuries. They were prideful and jealous, they had too many human attributes. As the decades passed, the witches began to fear the dragons. They started to hunt them, wanting to be at the top of the food chain."

The words left my lips before I could stop them. "And why wouldn't they mind link like you have with Freya?"

"The witches were too weak. They would have never survived the transition. Freya would have been ripped apart if she had been too weak." She retook a deep breath, and just like that, she was Freya. Her eyes returned back to their almost normal state of reptilian, and she gave me a small smile.

"Well, I guess I don't need to be the teacher here, now do I?" I leaned back and crossed my arms.

Her face burned red, and she looked down at Vailen with a scowl. "I'm sorry, I want to learn from you, but Vailen felt like he needed to step in for a moment." She bit her lip. "What about the first witch?"

"That's a little simpler." I let out a nervous laugh. But history was a good place to start before we got started on magic and potions and the like. "Have you ever heard of Merlin?"

Her mouth dropped open, and she leaned forward, curious about what I was about to disclose. "Go on."

"If I'm going to start anywhere, I have to start with the war. It was the War of Darkness." I licked my lips. Vailen perked up a bit on the floor, listening to what I had to say next. "It threw The Mirror

Realm into darkness and disease. It's not really a secret that the druids, what they were called before, and the elves had it out for each other. There was constant war, and I have no doubt, there is still strife among both lands. The elves won and forced Merlin and Morgana to the barren lands. Merlin fell in love with one of the princesses, and she allowed him to live. Morgana became bitter in the barren lands and promised to get revenge. He had left her to rot and didn't look back. He had only cared about himself. With her bitterness, she learned many things through her magic and befriended the creatures that had been banished with her. She rose up as the Queen of the Damned, and she broke free with all of her misfits behind her." I paused again and shook my head. "I don't know much else, but that somehow Merlin escaped or his children did and they came here. I'm sure there is more information on it in The Mirror Realm, but we may never know it."

Her jaw dropped open. "That's it? You leave me hanging like that? Like a stupid cliffhanger in a book." She pouted and leaned back in her chair, she folded her feet under her and then a mischievous twinkle lit up her eyes. "I think I have an idea."

I frowned. "I'm supposed to be teaching you,

and the look in your eye says that you want to find trouble."

She flipped her hair over her shoulder, almost as if she was reminding me that she was indeed a redhead. "It'll be fun. Plus, there are too many ears here."

She winked at me, and I had a feeling I was about to get into a lot of trouble with my father if I didn't keep us on track, but since when did I care what my father thought? "Fine."

She grabbed my hand and shot out of her chair. I grabbed the backpack from under Vailen, much to his disapproval, and let her drag me away. The librarian *shhh'ed* us as we flew by her, but Freya didn't have a care to give. We were in her room before I knew it and I was starting to get nervous. Which wasn't like me at all. I was the one that relished in the thought of being in a girl's bedroom. I dreamed of all the mischief my sister and I could get into. But, when it came to Freya, I was a bit more cautious. I closed the door softly behind me and observed as Freya yanked a bag from under her bed. It looked very similar to the one I had in my hand. Eerily similar.

"What's that?" I narrowed my eyes at her suspiciously.

"Wyna gave it to me." She looked at it like it was a bag of snakes. "I'm surprised you don't recognize it, especially with all that spying that you did."

"I probably missed it because I had gotten up to get popcorn, or maybe entertain a date. You pretend I don't have a sex life." I scoffed. She narrowed her eyes at me and scowled.

"I didn't bring you here so you could try to make me jealous." She rolled her eyes and finally stuck her hand in the mouth of the bag. Her entire arm disappeared, then her shoulder. She made a face of concentration, but before I knew it, she slipped in and was gone.

Why didn't I see this coming?

Down the rabbit hole, *I went.*

I was an idiot. Of course, this was probably a trap. I gigged as I fell down, *down, down.* What I would give to see Sterling's face right now. He was probably freaking out. I tried to imagine it as I continued down the fall.

I landed on a pile of clothes on my butt and looked around curiously. I wondered if I had made it to The Mirror Realm or if I had gone to Wonderland instead.

"What in Merlin's name?" I heard a voice squeak. I popped my head out of the clothes, and there she was, just a few inches tall with her hair in space buns. This time her hair was bright purple, and she had glitter roots. *Wyna.* She was wearing a tight corset with a loose blouse underneath and what looked to be leggings. "What are you doing here?" she whispered.

"I definitely didn't think this was possible," I muttered.

"How did you get here?" She closed the double doors behind her and gave me a nervous glance. "You are real, aren't you?"

I nodded my head. "I don't know how I got here. I was looking in the bag you gave me, trying to figure out how to get some books from the library and in I fell."

"Leave it to me to accidentally open a portal in a bag." She giggled, and it sounded like bells jingling. Then she got serious. "You can't be here. It's not safe."

"How do I get back?" I asked.

"Was someone with you when you opened the bag?"

"Yes," I said.

"Then chances are, they will more than likely reach in here to find you. You can use their magic as a tether to pull yourself free." Wyna bit her lip nervously. "You really can't be here though, and we really shouldn't be speaking. If Queen Armia finds out how to get to you and your world, she will do whatever it takes. Fortunately, this is a one-way portal."

"Because she is working with my mother, right?" Just as the words left my mouth, I felt the pull. Something in my soul was being yanked toward the ceiling, and then it opened up, and I could see Sterling's face. His face was everything I imagined it to be. It was pure terror as his eyes searched the darkness of the bag.

Wyna nodded. "There is too much magic going on right now. Lift your hand up, and you will go back home. Next time, put your hand in the bag and imagine what you want from it. It will come to you, and it will be my magic helping you. Don't try anything too scheme-y, I need to stay on the Queen's good side. I'll send you a letter when we can talk next." She floated over to me and pulled my finger into the air. She was a lot stronger than she looked.

`When she released me, my body shot up and out of the portal. I hit Sterling in the chest, and we both sprawled out on the floor. I shoved off of his chest.

Sterling wasn't having it though. He wrapped his arms around me and yanked me back down onto him. He flicked his pointer finger at the door, and I heard the latch of the lock take place.

Chills went up my spine as he pushed his hands into my already wild hair. I licked my lips nervously, and it must have fueled him, he pulled my head down to his, and I could feel his warm breath on my damp lips.

"You have this habit of leaving at the worst times," he growled. "For once, I'm going to stop being a gentleman, and I'm going to show you just how crazed you have made me."

I couldn't help but have a retort for that. "Gentleman? Since when?"

He didn't reply and devoured my lips. I couldn't keep up with his hungry endeavor, but I tried my best. My stomach dipped as he rolled us over and pinned me against the floor. My breathing was getting heavier, and I could feel his racing heart under the palm of my hand. His mouth left my lips and traveled down my cheek, to my jaw and then down my neck. I squeezed my eyes closed tighter and threw my head back to give him better access.

The sound of someone turning the doorknob had us scrambling apart, even though the door was locked. I buried my face in my hands and turned away.

"You two have too much sexual tension. That was interesting. Ayre is waiting outside the door." Vailen's voice in my mind made me jump, and I blushed harder. The dragon was still lazily laying on my bed with his eyes just barely open like he was bored and waiting for a snooze.

"Are you changing, Freya? If not, I'm coming in." Right on cue, the door burst open. Ayre was standing with both hands in the air and her palms facing us. Sterling was still seated on the floor, but instead of embarrassed, he was smirking.

Gentleman, ha!

Ayre looked at me, then at Sterling and then back and forth for about a minute, assessing the situation. "I think I interrupted something."

I said "No!" At the same time, Sterling said, "Yes!"

Ayre raised her eyebrows in an all-knowing look and then grinned. "I always wanted a sister."

"Oh. My. Gosh." I turned away from them both and hid my face in the side of the bed. I couldn't acknowledge or even think of that statement implied.

"My sister in law, the High Priestess!" she squealed.

I peeked at Sterling, and he threw a wink my way. *Oh, the nerve.*

I cleared my throat and decided to change the subject. "I fell into a portal."

Sterling's face lost all color. "You say that with too much confidence."

"I spoke to Wyna."

Ayre didn't even blink. "How is this possible?"

I pulled the bag my way and rubbed the straps between my fingers, thoughtfully. "She spelled this bag to be linked to a closet, so all the clothes I had while I was there, I would be able to wear here too. I'm sure there are other reasons the bag was spelled, but I don't know if she meant it to be an actual portal or not."

"Um, and you trust her?" Ayre frowned at me.

"I don't know, she said it's a one-way portal and that I wasn't safe there." I shrugged.

"Well, duh!" She went to take the backpack from me, and I yanked it from her reach. "We have to destroy that."

Sterling was watching us with curious eyes and an amused smirk on his lips.

"Are you going to back me on this?" Ayre asked him.

He shook his head. "I won't make a move

against our High Priestess, especially when she isn't in control of her powers yet."

Ayre sat back on her heels and pouted. "The Council won't like this."

"The Council won't know about this," Sterling said. He clenched his jaw, the amusement leaving his face.

"They are supposed to know about all open portals between worlds." Ayre gave her brother a glare.

"I can assure you that The Council doesn't know about all of the portals open between Realms. What do you want? We have studies we need to go over." Sterling pulled himself off of the ground and rolled up the stiff starch sleeves of his button down.

"Studies…" She trailed off and narrowed her eyes. "Of what? Human anatomy? I am not oblivious to what was happening in here."

"You will pretend to be." Sterling straightened his shirt and stood up tall. "It will be your best interest in doing so."

He was all business, and something about his demeanor reminded me of Jonathan. Like father, like son.

He turned his head from side to side, cracking his neck before he extended his hand to me and helped me from the floor. "I know you don't want to discuss what happens in Liam's quarters, so you will be wise to keep quiet what happens in ours."

Ayre turned bright pink, rolled her eyes and straighten herself up, ready to take on her brother. "You will be wise to watch who you speak to with that tone. I was friends with Freya first. You will not act like Father to get your way."

He shrunk back at her words. His jaw clenched and unclenched as he thought of the words to retaliate.

I interjected. "We will catch up later." I put my hand on her shoulder and smiled, to remind her that I wasn't the enemy here. "We will have a lot of things to discuss, and I'm sure I'll have more questions. Questions that your brother won't answer." I winked at her, and her face softened. Something was bothering her, I could feel it, but when she pulled away the feeling was gone. Ayre left the room with her head held high, scowling at her brother until the door closed between us.

"So much for locks," Sterling muttered.

"I'm sure you could use magic next time." I winked.

He grabbed my hand and pulled me to him. "So, there's going to be a next time?"

It was my turn to wink.

He sat in the chair by the window and got comfortable. "We have a lot of work to do, and if I want to have more fun with you, we need to finish soon."

I tried to ignore his words, but I couldn't ignore the effect they had on my body. It was a foreign feeling, and I was enjoying it too much to deny.

"I want to know about the different creatures in New Orleans," I said a matter of fact.

He scratched at the stubble on his face and began the lesson. "There is our New Orleans coven of witches, as you know. Some live with us here in the compound, and some live in their own homes. We all pull from the essence here in the Quarter." I had questions on the tip of my tongue about other High Priestesses in the area, but I didn't need to stop him. I was finally getting answers. "There are werewolves in the bayou. You met one of the packs, The Heberts. There are also Vampires, they only come out for the tourists and parties on the weekend. They mostly reside in the 9th ward. They rule the people there. They keep some order to the area, but some would disagree and say that there is none there."

I leaned forward from my seat, listening intently.

He continued, "Obviously there are dragons. We had always thought they were extinct, but now I am not so sure." He paused and gazed at Vailen cuddling the other egg. "As far as I know, mermaids aren't real. I always thought that Rougarrous weren't real either. I guess I have been wrong before." He laughed softly. "Fairies don't exist in our realm, though a few have escaped their own and have come here, just to be hunted and killed by the humans. Shapeshifters have been a common topic in our history book, but I haven't met one yet. At least not that I know of."

"Are we friends of most of these creatures?" I asked, hesitantly.

"For the most part, yes. My mother loved to befriend anyone and everyone, she tried to keep the peace between our races as much as she could. More times than not, these other groups need us, not really the other way around." He waggled his eyebrows at me, trying to make the conversation light.

"So, the witches are apart of the food chain, so to speak?" I asked.

"Yes and no." He scratched his face. "The Vampires could hold more power if they wanted to, but they are night-walkers. Night-walkers have a

CHAPTER 15 | 123

hard time gaining control over much. The were-wolves were once royalty here, but feuds with the Vampires drove them into the swamps. We could talk about their history all night, but it isn't that important."

"Why do we need potions if we can use the essence to use magic? Why do we need spells if we have our magis?"

Sterling thought about it for a second. "The magic is within you." He touched my face tenderly. "When you use your magi, spells, and potions... You are pulling from the extra magic. The extra magic in the essence, from the ancestors, and things like that. You are only so powerful. Everyone needs a little help."

"Are there other High Priestesses in New Orleans or even in Louisiana?" I bit my lip.

"There aren't."

I frowned. "What do you mean?"

"We said you were the High Priestess of the New Orleans coven because we didn't want to over-whelm you with your future responsibilities. To be completely honest, we didn't think you would become High Priestess so soon. My mother thought she would have time to better prepare you for this position."

I scowled. I could feel my temper flaring like a flame. "And yet, she hasn't really spoken to me once about any of it."

"My mother loves to give space. She wants you to figure out what you can on your own and when you have done all you can, to come to her." He looked down at the rug and pressed his lips together.

"So, I am the High Priestess to all of Louisiana?" I swallowed. *No pressure.*

"Yes." He wouldn't look me in the eye. "But, no."

"How vague of you." I crossed my arms over my chest. I wasn't doing well with this study session. My temper was growing hot inside of my chest I didn't know how much more of his evasiveness I could take.

"The essence is in New Orleans, most witches don't venture out past because their magic grows weak unless they go to another state to a larger coven. There are smaller covens or witch huts around Louisiana, but they have very little power. That's why we have so many that live and stay here in the compound."

"How many High Priestesses are there?"

"You ask more questions than a toddler." He

chuckled. I scowled more.

"There are probably 10 in the United States. There are more in other countries." He unrolled his shirt sleeve, then rolled it back up. He had a nervous fidget. "You will only find witches where there are big amounts of energy. New York, Miami, San Fransisco, Salt Lake, Chicago, Dallas, Nashville and there are a few others that I don't really know off the top of my head. The essence essentially feeds off of the high energy in those places and then, in turn, let's us borrow it."

I guessed that made sense. I was soaking it all in, trying to imagine it.

"Why was Sariah kicked out of being the High Priestess when she fled New Orleans? She only went to the swamp." This was the question that had been eating at me, the question that I had been too afraid to ask.

"I have a theory." Sterling paused.

"Let's hear it." I stopped scowling to encourage him to continue. I really needed to work on my patience with people. How could I lead anyone if I felt all panicky and explosive when answers were taking too long?

"I think your mother gave it up."

"Please," I closed my eyes. "Please, do not call her that."

"Very well." I could hear him shifting in his chair. I had probably made him uncomfortable, but what was I to do? Be uncomfortable in his place? That's probably what a good High Priestess would do for her people. "I think she released her hold on it."

"I could do that?" I looked down at my hands. At my magi.

"No," I looked up at him. He was staring at my eyes. "Only if you had a daughter that you could pass it to. If you were in danger, or on your death bed. I'm not sure of the technicalities. Maybe she sensed that you were in danger or maybe the essence was done with her. We may never know what happened."

I touched my neck. The bruises were gone, but I could still see them in my mind. Had Sariah given me this huge burden to save my life?

"Okay, so what now?"

"Now you will be introduced to the coven at the ball, and we will move your lessons to the study."

I whipped my head up. "Why can't we do it here?"

The corner of his mouth quirked up. "As much

as I love the thought of it. I'm afraid the only thing you would be learning is the shape of me…" He rose up from his chair. I could barely hear the lock clicking into place once more. My heart pounded in my ears, drowning out the sound of anything else. His face was now inches from mine. "The taste of me…" His lips brushed mine. "The feel of me…" His hands grasped my waist, and he pulled me from the chair. I wrapped my legs around his waist and stared, wide-eyed at him. His eyes were heavy with lust as his lips captured mine again.

When he pulled away, I couldn't put together a coherent thought. "What if I would rather learn those things?" I whispered, breathlessly.

"I always wondered why I pushed you away so much, now I know." His eyes searched mine. "Something inside of me knew that you would be the beginning of my demise."

CHAPTER SIXTEEN

I replayed the day before over and over in my mind. I didn't know what had come over me. I had been wanton with desire and no matter what I did, I couldn't stop wanting more. I kept pushing my boundaries and Freya's little by little. What had started out innocent had taken a turn rather quickly.

I grasped the sides of the vanity in my bathroom and stared at the granite. I was getting way in over my head. I had to play hot and heavy with Shay to keep the charade up, but behind closed doors, the only person I was getting hot and heavy with was Freya. I splashed cold water on my face and gazed at myself in the mirror. I was getting myself tangled up quickly, and if I wanted to get out of this alive, I needed to plan and strategize better. I was going to have to stop whatever was brewing between Freya and I. I was starting down a path of no return.

A knock at the door pulled me from my thoughts. I turned the water off and yanked the door open. My mood was apparent on my face. Shay took a step back and tried to smile. "Are you okay?"

"I'm fine," I muttered and pushed past her.

"You don't look or seem fine." She caught up with me and rested her hand on my back.

I whipped around and grabbed her wrist and pushed her against the wall. "I said, I'm fine." I threw her hand from my grasp, and she immediately cradled it against her chest, while giving me a scared look. I took a deep breath. "I'm sorry, I shouldn't be taking this out on you."

"What happened?" Shay asked.

Then it hit me. I could see the plan formulating in my mind. I knew exactly what I was going to do. "Freya pushed me to my breaking point yesterday."

Shay's eyebrows pulled together in concern. "What do you mean?"

"I can't work with her anymore. I don't think

she belongs as High Priestess." The words left my mouth bitterly.

Her eyebrows drew apart then rose up her forehead in surprise. "What do you want to do?"

"I can't put this on you. I shouldn't have even said anything." I turned away from her and pressed my forehead against the wall. I could hear Freya in the other room speaking to Ayre, I couldn't tell what they were discussing, but I could hear her sweet voice. It would torment me for the weeks to come. It would haunt me in my dreams because what I was about to do was blasphemy.

Shay touched my back again, and I could feel the revulsion rolling through my body. I couldn't stand the person I was about to become, just for knowledge, just to protect Freya. "You can tell me anything."

I clenched my hands into fists. "I've been conspiring against my father."

She pulled away as if I burned her. "What does that even mean?" She sounded horrified, and for a moment, I was worried. Had I said the wrong thing? Had I taken this too far?

"I knew I shouldn't have said anything." I pushed away from the wall and didn't look her way as I made my way to the dresser. I yanked a duffle bag from the bottom drawer and started to throw random clothes into the bag. I needed this to look like it was exactly how it looked, last minute and thrown together. I didn't care what I was putting the bag, that wasn't what this was about.

"I don't know where your loyalties lie, but I can't stay here." I turned around and looked her in the eyes. "I'm leaving tonight."

"What?" Her eyes grew round, and she grabbed my arms to make me stop and look at her. "What happened yesterday? I heard Ayre bust up in your study session with Freya, and she left all pissy, but I thought that was just typical sibling rivalry."

"Freya used magic to seduce me last night."

Deadpanned. That was the only way to describe her face. Shock, then confusion took over. "I thought she needed help with her magic."

"Yeah, well, turns out that she doesn't."

"I thought you were *the* womanizer." She was trying to make light of the conversation or trying to break me, it didn't work.

"Yeah, there's nothing like magic to set the mood," I said, sarcastically.

Her face softened. "I'm sorry. Where are you going to go?"

"I have some friends in the Nashville coven," I

muttered, as I threw the closet door open. It bounced off of the wall with a bang. Shay flinched.

"You aren't going to think this through?" She tried to stop me again.

"Nope." I threw a few pairs of shoes onto the clothes mushed together in chaos.

"I have a place," Shay said. I turned around and narrowed my eyes at her.

"What is that supposed to mean?" Suspicion filled my voice, even though I knew what she was about to say.

"There's a witch hut down the block." She whispered, even though we were alone. She bit her nail nervously before she continued. "It's where outlaws go."

"That must have been where Liam mentioned."

"Liam has been there before, but the only way you'll be allowed in…" She bit her lip. "is if you renounce your Priestess."

Was I willing to go that far for a ruse? "I'm willing to do that. Freya will be the downfall of our coven. She's too weak."

I wanted to stop and leave Freya a note, or my parents, but I knew it was too risky. I couldn't take any chances with what I was about to embark on.

"Put your bag under your bed. The sun isn't

down yet, and I need to gather my things. Take what's important to you. We won't be returning. Act normal."

I could do that. She kissed my mouth and was out the door. I pushed the bed away from the wall and pried one of the boards from the floor. This was where I kept my illegal potions and brews. The things that my father let me horde. He knew because he had left the drawer unlocked so many times and left me alone in there with a wink as a farewell.

As much as I despised my father, I knew he wanted more from me. I had explosives, and sleeping droughts, but what I needed was in a pouch at the very bottom. I didn't know if it would put a dragon to sleep, but I hoped to the ancestors it would do the trick. It would be my last prayer to them when I renounced my service from my Priestess, I would lose their favor. I didn't know if I would ever get it back either. But I did realize I needed to keep Freya safe and this was the only way I could do it.

I waited until I knew Ayre and Freya had gone downstairs and found my little crawl space in the closet. I grasped the powder tightly in my hands, my fingers trembling slightly. When I pushed through Freya's clothes, Vailen was waiting for me in the doorway of the closet. I had to act quickly, Vailen was sly and cunning. He knew what I was coming for. No doubt he had heard me speaking to Shay through the walls.

"I'm sorry that I have to do this. Tell Freya, maybe someday those lessons will be within my grasp, and I'll be worthy." I didn't wait for the words to register, I threw the powder in Vailen's face and whispered, "*Crésent.*"

His body collapsed at my feet. He would be out for maybe a few minutes, and I knew Freya would be here soon. She would feel the connection of her familiar bond flexing with the spell.

The white dragon egg laid on the bed. I scooped it up and dropped it into my sock. I didn't know how I was going to conceal this thing for the witch hut, but I needed to be smart. I rubbed my thumb and my pointer finger together over the sock, and my magi cooled on my chest. The egg disappeared and turned into a wad of cash before my eyes. Illusions were my favorite trick. I had practiced them since my magic had started to manifest. Ayre had been my favorite target.

I left the doors open, they needed to know it was me. I didn't understand why I was hell-bent on closing my own coffin, but if it didn't point to me, the guilt would eat me alive.

I shoved my bed back into place, not worried with putting the floorboard back and grabbed my duffle bag after I pushed the egg at the bottom. I rushed from my room and passed Freya on my way down. Her eyes were full of concern, but she wasn't focused on me. She was determined to get to her beast, that was unconscious in the closet. She would mind link with him soon enough and know everything.

I let myself into Shay's room. She was pushing her stuff into a bag, and when she turned around, she had a throwing knife ready to go. "Sorry, old habit."

I cocked an eyebrow. Interesting old habit to have. "We have to leave."

"We can't leave until dark." She pulled the curtain open and showed me that it was still indeed very much day time outside.

"Now. I'm serious." I demanded.

"What did you do?" She looked at the door behind me and shook her head. "I promised I wouldn't do this to them. But it sounds like chaos out there, we have no choice." She waved her right hand in a circle and picked up her bag in her left hand. Wind started to spin around us. When she dropped her hand, we were no longer in her room. We were in a bar and not a bar I had ever been to. The smoke was heavy above us, and I could smell blood in the air. We were in a Blood Bar, not a witch hut.

"You know better than to do that shit around here, Shay." The bartender barked. "Who do you have with you?" The bartender was a tall, woman. All limbs with a crop top and micro shorts.

"It was an emergency." Her accent was stronger than I had ever heard it. "We have business to attend to."

The bartender put the glass down that she was cleaning. "Are you back for good, or just for business?"

"We're back for good, *love*." Her smile was predatory. "Let Ricky know we are here."

Shay grabbed my hand and led me to a table in the back. It was dark, and I could hardly see where I was walking. "If there is anything you need to confess, you need to tell me now."

I leaned back and frowned. "And what would I need to confess?"

"Anything you don't want to come up with a truth serum. Ricky isn't one for mercy."

"If you think I'm too dumb to not know this, then maybe I should find another place to hang out. When you said outlaw, I knew there would be repercussions. I am not here for games or fun, I am here because I don't believe what the covens are preaching anymore. I don't think Freya should be the Priestess and I don't like games." I spit out.

I could see her teeth glow in the dark as she smiled. "Good, good. I'm sure you won't have any problem with Ricky then."

"I'm sure I won't." I crossed my arms over my chest.

"They're ready for us," She grabbed my arm and the booth we had been standing near disappeared, and a door appeared in its place. When we passed through the door, the light from the new room was blinding. I leaned forward and blinked my eyes several times. Shay didn't seem fazed by it.

"Welcome back, Priestess." A man said from across the room. He was sprawled out on a leather couch with a beer in his hand. There were many people in the room, most of them wearing leather and drinking.

Shay's cheeks turned pink, and she brushed off what he was saying. "Hey, Ricky. This is-"

"Ole' Sterling Masters, what are you doing here,

boy?" The man's southern accent was sharp as he pushed himself up into a sitting position, knocked back the rest of the beer and stood up. Ricky pushed his sandy blond hair from his face and made his way toward me. With Ricky's attention on me, many others started to turn my way too.

"Shay told me she had a place for me to stay, but she didn't mention it was a blood bar." I stared into his lavender eyes. I was looking for a challenge.

"You here to shut us down, boy?" Ricky cocked his head and cackled. Shay intertwined her fingers with mine. "Ohhhh, Priestess got a boyfriend. How cute." Ricky's eyes went cold and dead.

"Sterling is my guest. We are here to seek sanctuary." I wanted to look at her but I couldn't. Declaring sanctuary was only something a High Priestess could do. This was not good.

"You promised you wouldn't pull that stuff here, Shay." Ricky pulled a toothpick from his pocket.

"If you call me Priestess then I will act like one." Shay lifted her chin. "You know the rules."

"I only have one room," Ricky spit at our feet. Shay narrowed her eyes. "Boss is going to want to see him."

"So be it." Shay snarled. "Tell us where we are staying."

. . .

I PACED THE FLOOR. It was starting to become my thing apparently. The room they showed us to was clean enough. Shay sat on the bed wringing her hands. "You requested sanctuary."

"Yes," Shay whispered. She wouldn't look up at me.

"Tell me it doesn't mean what I think it means."

"I wish I could." She brushed her hair from her face and still kept her eyes on the stained carpet. "I wanted to tell you, I just didn't know how."

Things were just getting foggier and foggier. All a coincidence, my ass.

"Who is the boss?" I asked.

"His name is Axel. He came with me here to New Orleans not very long ago. I don't know much about him, but he is looking for revenge against someone here. Well, your old coven." She looked up at the floor, and her eyes held too much concern.

"You're the future Priestess of the Paris coven, aren't you?" It made sense. Now that I was putting the pieces together, I remembered that her mother had the same black hair and figure. I had met her once when I was still studying at the institute.

"It's not something I want people to know."

"And why not?" My frown deepened.

"Because people treat you differently."

I knew that all too well. I couldn't blame her, but I also knew one thing. I didn't trust her, and I wasn't about to start now.

I WAS STARING at the ceiling when the door swung open. I didn't even move. It was probably one of Ricky's goons. Though, I didn't know why they would be coming in here. Shay had declared sanctuary, so that meant they weren't allowed to truth serum either of us. I didn't know why she had done it, but I imagined it was to protect herself. She was protecting her demons, and I was defending my lies.

Shay scrambled from the bed and stood up. I tried not to roll my eyes as I looked to the door. But standing in the doorway was someone unmistakeable, and I blinked hard. I sat up, not believing my eyes.

"Hello, Sterling." The man said.

"Hello, Cullen." I had no doubt in my mind of who he was.

He chuckled. "I don't really go by that anymore."

"Let me guess, Axel?" I asked.

"I feel like it suits me a little better." He leaned against the wall, and I was really able to get a good look at him. His red hair was long and wavy past his ears while it hung just over his eyes. He was long and tall, the complete opposite of his twin.

"I don't think that's the case." I tilted my head slightly.

"Oh? What is it then?"

"I think you are afraid of people knowing who you really are. Honestly, the red hair and black eyes should have given you away to anyone in New Orleans, but I guess, they are in denial. Not only did Sariah's daughter live, but so did her son."

CHAPTER SEVENTEEN

FREYA

Chaos was the only way to describe it. Enforcers were storming the building. Something had triggered alarms after I had found Vailen unconscious in the closet.

Ayre explained to me that when there is a breach in the protective wards around the coven, it will sound alarms. Enforcers come to make sure that everyone is safe and to reprimand the person in charge of the dark magic within. But they were already gone. Shay and Sterling. Everything had happened in minutes.

I remembered seeing him pass me on the stairs, but now as I thought back on it. His eyes had been saying goodbye. Pain clutched my heart and tormented me. I didn't want to believe that it could be true. I rocked back and forth on the bed, waiting for Vailen to wake up. Ayre let out a scream of frustration in Sterling's room. She was finding it empty, and she didn't want to believe it either.

The way he had touched me and kissed me was still fresh in my mind. It kept playing on a loop. I hugged the blanket to my chest and tried to keep it together. I just didn't understand.

"Do you think this is part of an act?" Ayre whispered from the doorway. I unfolded myself from the bed and covers that were keeping me comforted and put together. I made my way to her slowly, like she was an injured animal. She collapsed in my arms when I got to her. "Do you think he will come back?" I looked at my slumbering dragon for reassurance, but I was afraid too. *What had he done to Vailen?*

"*Do not fret, Priestess. He wanted the other dragon egg. He wanted my a mate.*" Vailen said, weakly in my mind.

"Your mate?" I spoke the words out loud and practically dragged Ayre to the bed. We both tumbled to the floor in front of my waking monster.

"*Yes, most of the time, our scales match the color of our eggs. It's not a coincidence that that color egg would come forth after my rebirth.*"

"What do I do?" My lips trembled. His mate was retaken from him.

"*Press your forehead against mine.*"

I did as he commanded and the scene played over before me. I heard what he said through the wall while I had been too busy hearing about Ayre's date with Liam. Tears filled my eyes. I tried to remember what he said about not buying his act when he was with Shay, but then he left. His eyes would torment me when he told Vailen, "*Maybe someday those lessons will be within my grasp, and I'll be worthy.*"

Ayre hugged me close and we just sat there until Jonathan and Cassie came in the room and pulled us apart. "Sterling and Shay were seen in a blood bar on Bourbon."

Ayre shot up from the floor. "Are we going to get him?"

"Sterling is an adult, and he hasn't done anything wrong." Cassie looked so sad as she spoke. "He has renounced Freya as his High Priestess."

I was confused. *Was that a thing? What did that even mean?* My questions must have been apparent because Jonathan started to explain, "You have a bond with all the people in your coven, you will come to feel it stronger as you get to know the members and work with them. When someone renounces you, it takes that bond away, permanently. These bonds serve a purpose in you helping keep the coven together and safe."

"When I touched Ayre earlier, I felt her sadness and pain and when she pulled away, I no longer felt that."

Cassie nodded. "Your empathy is stronger now, especially when you are around those that you have deep connections with."

I replayed what Vailen heard through the walls.

Freya used magic to seduce me last night.

It hadn't been on purpose. I didn't know about this bond.

My eyes filled up with more tears that threatened to spill over. How had I not known? It hadn't been real. I blinked my eyes several times, trying to keep it together. I was the damn High Priestess. I couldn't fall apart over a silly boy.

"He left because of me and this bond. He told Shay I tried to seduce him with magic. That I know more of what I am doing than I let on." I sniffled and almost fell apart again. But even as I felt myself falling apart, I also felt myself coming together. Who was he to say those things about me? Who was he to revert back? Who was he to treat me like this again?

"This isn't your fault." Cassie put her hand on my shoulder to comfort me, but it just made it worse. Her sorrow over her son was flowing at me like huge waves. Each one that crashed into me was stronger than the last. I broke the embrace and wrapped my arms around myself.

"That doesn't even sound like Sterling." Jonathan leaned against the wall and shook his head. "He would love it if a woman tried to seduce him. Why? Because it would mean that he wouldn't have to."

"You're right," Ayre wiped under her eyes. "That doesn't sound like him. Sterling is a lot of things, but he has chemistry with you, Freya. He genuinely likes you. There's another agenda here that we aren't seeing."

I wanted to believe them, but the pain in my heart was a lot to handle. As well as my temper. Pain and stubbornness both had a tight hold on me. I nodded and wrapped my arms around Vailen. I could feel his pain for his mate through our bond.

"I *am deeply saddened because I want to be the first thing she sees if she comes back to me. But I know that Sterling will not harm her. She is in the best care, and he wouldn't have taken her unless he knew he needed her. He is headed into dangerous waters and uncharted territory. There is no telling what is to come from this."* Vailen's pep talked helped a little, but not as much as I needed.

Ayre climbed up into my bed and pulled the covers around herself. Jonathan opened the door for Cassie, and they left, knowing that nothing they did or said would help me feel any better. The only thing that would help was time and maybe, answers.

"I HAVE AN IDEA," Ayre whispered to me in the dark an hour later.

My eyes shot open. "I feel like this is going to be a bad idea."

"I think Liam knows where they are, like can really get us into the Blood Bar." Ayre whispered back.

"And what are we going to do? Go on a rescue mission?" I asked.

"Yep." She sounded way too confident. She had been plotting since I had turned off the lights.

"What if he doesn't want to be rescued?"

"Then we will drag him home kicking and

screaming." I could almost hear Ayre smiling in the dark.

"I feel like this is a really bad idea." I laughed.

"You're probably right." She still sounded confident. "We're still doing it."

I rolled my eyes and tried to go to sleep. I was going to need as much rest as I could possibly get.

I COULD HEAR Ayre screaming through the door. "WHAT DO YOU MEAN YOU CAN'T HELP US?" At this rate, the entire coven would know what we were up to. I knocked on the door, but it still didn't stop Ayre's tirade against her poor love interest. "I swear on my ancestors if you don't tell me-"

She was cut off, so I pushed the door open and laughed at what I saw. Liam couldn't talk any sense into her, so he shut her up with his lips. *How typical.*

Ayre pulled away with a smack and scowled at me. "What are you doing? I told you to wait outside."

"What are you doing? You are announcing your espionage to the entire coven, and I'm pretty sure you horrified a few families when you swore on the ancestors." I folded my arms and gave her an incredulous look.

"I'm trying to get my answers. It's hard work." She dusted off Liam's shoulder and gave me a sly look. "I don't recommend it. It's not easy getting what you want."

For a moment I wished I had just stayed upstairs with Vailen and sulked in bed all day. I sighed. It was going to be a long day.

CHAPTER EIGHTEEN

STERLING

C ullen's smile was a predator's grin. "I've heard our resemblance is uncanny, but I'm not brave enough to approach her coven, not yet at least."

"It's a little shocking, but even I can enjoy a plot twist," I smirked.

"What are you doing here, Sterling? Last I heard you had it out for my sister. Wouldn't you like to keep enemies close? Or is that what you're doing now?" I couldn't take my eyes off of his. It was like he was dead. They were just pits inside his head, and they unnerved me, but I couldn't look away.

"I don't trust your sister." I lied.

"I don't trust her either." He smiled again.

"Really? So, that's why you haven't come to

visit? Or is it the black magic running through your veins? Sariah would be so proud. Following like a little puppy, right in her own footsteps."

That got him. He flew across the room and wrapped his fingers around my neck. It was my turn to smile. I struggled to get the words out, "Is this how you killed her?"

His hand tightened, but I remained firm. My magi knew how to play this game. Ayre and I had competed on who could hold their breath for the longest over our long summer breaks in the pool. My magi had caught on quick and helped me, Ayre's had not, and she had almost drowned one year. He squeezed and squeezed until he didn't get the reaction he was looking for and let me go.

"I don't divulge my secrets to new members." Cullen looked me up and down. "And if I had wanted to kill her, she would still be dead." He shoved me away from him and walked out of the room.

Shay rushed to my side and touched my neck tenderly. "Are you okay?"

I smiled down at her. "Yes, I'm fine."

"How did you do that? You stayed conscious without oxygen for a solid few minutes." Her eyes were huge as she fussed over me.

"I need you to be honest with me." I looked into her eyes. "How do you know him?"

She looked at the floor. "He came to my coven about a year ago. My father saw his eyes and told him to never return. My mother, however, didn't agree and did a truth scrum on him. His answers were clean, so my mom let him stay. We became fast friends, and then lovers. My father forbids us to be together, and that was when he left. I only knew him as Axel. I ran away with him." She shook her head, a faraway look in her eye. "It's unheard of for the future High Priestess to leave. My mom let me go. She said that I would return with wisdom. My father told me not to ever come back, that they could have another daughter that would serve her duty." She blinked and looked at the wall. Her eyes grew glassy, and I didn't know if it was fake or not. "When I got here, everything changed. Axel no longer wanted me unless I was willing to run errands for him and they kept including your coven."

"Go on." I encouraged softly when she stopped speaking.

"As I sat there and watched the exchange, I realized that I was just a pawn in his scheme. He didn't even look my way." She tried to smile, but I could still see the pain there. "I now see that I don't belong here."

"What are you going to do?" I knew I could make it here without her, but I didn't know exactly how I was going to do it.

"I need to go back home if my father lets me, but I need to see this through first." She pointed to the bag. "Take the dragon egg out."

I lifted an eyebrow and snorted. "What? You know the last dragon is with Freya."

"I followed you to Madam Shriek's. I know you don't let the thing out of your sight. I also know that it was delivered for Axel or Cullen, whatever his name is." She looked at the door, cautiously. "I know how to awaken the dragon."

All I could do was stare at her.

"Axel told me about it, and when Freya came back with a dragon, we all knew it was heavy amounts of power... From a High Priestess. I was supposed to awaken the dragon for him. Just a pawn." Shay brushed her hair over her shoulder and went for my bag.

I lifted my hand up, in defense, ready to do what I would need to keep her away from it. "Consider your next moves wisely."

"If Axel finds out you have it, he will kill you.

His magic is unmatched. You need me to awaken it." She held her hands up in surrender.

"This wasn't apart of the plan," I said.

"Do you think any of this was apart of the plan?" She waved her hands around wildly. "You need me, and if you don't realize that, then you are not as smart as I thought you were."

"What am I supposed to do with a dragon? Here?"

"It's the only thing that will protect you when I am gone. Axel will not hesitate to kill me. I am nothing to him now." She ran for the bag and grabbed the wad of cash out before I could do anything. She threw it at me, and I caught it quickly. I held it at my chest, and before I could blink, Shay blasted me with a spell.

"I'm sorry." She whispered. The pain hit me in the chest. It felt like I had been shot. I fell to my knees and closed my eyes. She hit me with another spell, and I felt like I was dying.

Before I knew it, everything was wiped clean from around me. I was staring at nothing. Everything was white, and the only thing that mattered was what I was holding in my hands. Her tail was more significant than her body and was wrapped protectively around her body.

Her body was covered in iridescent scales, that shimmered pink and purple in the light. Her crystal blue eyes blinked up at me innocently. She was the size of my palm, but I knew with time she would be able to change her size at whim. Fire licked at my fingers as she tested her strength. But before I knew it, we were pulled from the void we had been placed in and back in the room at the blood bar.

"You don't have much time, you can conceal her, but I don't know how well you are at holding illusions," Shay said, standing above me. Somehow I had been knocked off of my feet, and I was laying flat on my back. The little dragon was curled up at my side, sleeping peacefully. "She trusts you."

I pulled my magi from my shirt and focused on the creature curled up beside me. Her image wavered for a moment before she turned into a white cat. She narrowed her eyes at me, and all I could do was shrug. Cats were healthy, right? I shoved her into my duffle bag, and she snuggled down into my clothes.

The door burst open, and I pushed my duffle bag under the bed with my foot. Cullen looked between Shay and me suspiciously. "I felt the magic being pulled. What's going on up here?"

Shay didn't miss a beat. "I was trying to kill his cat."

I glared at her before I looked back at Cullen. "She was trying to kill me."

Cullen's eyes flicked to my partially hidden bag behind my legs. Right on cue the little animal poked her head out and meowed. I didn't know if it was a good plan or not, but it was all I had. Cullen's eyebrows shot up to his hairline. "I'm surprised I didn't hear the thing in here before."

Shay gave him a bored look. "I told you I was trying to kill it."

Cullen gave her a bored look right back before he looked back at me. "Is it your familiar? I find it odd that you have a white cat as a familiar, but I have seen stranger things."

I nodded my head and tried to remain as submissive as possible even though everything in me wanted to challenge him.

"Very well, stop trying to kill his cat, Shay. There is no reason to be jealous." He turned to leave and stopped. "Even though the cat is prettier than you, I can understand how it could be confusing."

As much as I didn't like Shay, Cullen's words bothered me. Maybe it was because Shay had been vulnerable with me and I felt the need to protect her, or perhaps it was because I disliked Cullen more than anyone else. I obviously would feel pity for anyone he set his sites on negatively.

Shay stared at the door and didn't say a word before she shucked off her clothing and climbed under the covers. There was only one bed in the room, and I imagined that meant I would be sleeping on the floor. Shay went to remove her bra, and I turned away. I knew I had a role to play in all of this, but I couldn't take it that far. I wouldn't be able to forgive myself.

"You don't have to act like you like me anymore," Shay said.

"Oh?" I peeked over my shoulder, and she had the blankets pulled up to her chin.

"I'm not an idiot. We both needed out of your coven, and now I need out of here. I have seen the way you look at Freya." She looked down at the material covering herself. "I thought it was a little crush. Something that you would get over once she came back to you safe. But when she came back, you just got worse."

"Or better?"

She rolled her eyes. "You love her."

I laughed. "I wouldn't go that far."

"Someday you will realize it. She's it for you." Shay whispered.

"Why are you helping me?"

"You needed to know who killed her, but you had to come to me first. Liam is innocent you should know." Shay said.

"I already know. I did a truth serum on him." I sat on the bed and faced away from her.

"Huh, well, that makes sense. I thought you had been suspicious of me from the start."

"Not really. I actually liked you in the beginning until I figured out what you were doing." I replied.

"I don't really know what to do with myself now. I had thought Cullen would accept me back and now this. I need to go home." I heard her roll over and I didn't say anything back. She would need a distraction to get away, and I knew the perfect way to do it.

CHAPTER NINETEEN

L iam had broken hours ago. I didn't know what Ayre had done to get the answers, but then again, I didn't really want to know either. Liam was the one that had told the Master's where they were, but he wouldn't give them any more information. Ayre was a completely different story. It hadn't taken Ayre long, and we knew all about the blood bar, except who ran the thing. Liam didn't know his name, but he frightened him enough.

Liam grabbed at Ayre's hands. "You don't understand. You two can't go there alone. That would be suicide. The man that runs the blood bar and witch's hut, he's the one that sent to have you killed, Freya."

I turned back toward them and frowned. "What do you mean?"

"They are starting an uprising. They want to take you out of the hierarchy, permanently. If you and your mother die, the hierarchy will probably go back to Cassie Masters." Liam pushed his hands through his hair.

"You wanted me dead?" I marched my way to him. I poked his chest with every word. "You. Wanted. Me. Dead?"

"No." He flinched.

"Then what is it? You cannot be on the fence." I could feel my temper flaring. I bunched up his shirt in my fist and shoved him into the wall. Even though I was a good foot shorter than he was, I was surprised by my strength.

"I didn't want you to be our High Priestess, but I also didn't understand how it worked." He struggled against my grip, and I felt a hand on my back, trying to comfort me or calm me down, I didn't know. I released his shirt and took a step back.

"I thought that was common knowledge," I said.

"Not really. You're friends with the daughter of the temporary High Priestess. You never really hung out with the regular witches around the coven.

Of course, we are going to know more than just anyone. You have been a part of the inner circle since you got here."

Ayre linked her fingers through mine and pulled me away from Liam. "It's okay to be mad, but we are getting mad at the wrong people."

Since when was Ayre the voice of reason?

"She's right you know," Jonathan said from the doorway.

That's when.

"I want more than anything to tear in there and get my son, but we don't know his plan, and we have *no* plan." Jonathan continued. "We could get him killed. Especially if he is in there trying to find the person that had you killed."

I tried to push through the fog and pain of what Vailen had shown me; obviously Sterling had been trying to tell me something, and I was too stubborn and stuck in my own jealousy to see it. "He just had to leave with *her*."

"You're hilarious when you're jealous." Ayre laughed.

I rolled my eyes. Where was Vailen when I needed him to be scary and terrify everyone away from me?

Jonathan leaned against the closed door and

looked me in the eyes. "You two are forbidden to go after Sterling."

Liam was the first to speak up. "I'm pretty sure that you can't boss around the High Priestess."

Hehe, maybe Liam wasn't so bad. He had captured Ayre's heart.

"I am apart of the Council. I can do whatever I wish." Jonathan spat.

"Is there a handbook on all of this because I would love to find where it says that." I piped up.

Ayre motioned for me to cut it out, drawing a finger across her neck. But to her surprise and mine, Jonathan laughed. Ayre gave me an even weirder look and looked like she was ready to flee. I didn't blame her, but there was a reason Jonathan was leaning against the only exit in the room.

A portal would be nice right now. Ayre must have had the same thought because we locked eyes and Ayre lifted her hand and looked like she was about to blow a kiss. Everything happened quickly. She blew on her open palm. Liam grabbed me, and we all fell into the portal and were spit out in the middle of the Quarter.

A drunk mortal tripped over my legs and giggled. "Cool trick!"

"Literally the best thing about being a witch in

New Orleans, mostly everyone is so drunk that they think our magic is always a trick," Liam muttered from underneath me.

I scrambled up off of him and dusted myself off. Touching the pavement in New Orleans was a major sin. Rats, roaches, and feces were rampant on the streets.

"Yes, what a cool trick indeed." Sariah purred across the street. I took a step back, but then there she was, right next to me. Damn portals.

"What do you want and what are you doing here?" I asked, not in the mood for her or what she had to say.

"We need to talk." Sariah started.

"No, we don't." I grabbed Ayre's hand, who grabbed Liam's hand and we formed a line walking down Bourbon Street.

"You aren't prepared to go there," she called from behind us.

"What makes you think that?" I stopped, but I didn't turn around.

"You have the same power flowing through your veins," Sariah muttered.

I turned around then. "Speaking of which, why did you give me these? What on Earth were you thinking when you gave all this up to me?"

"I thought I could save you, unlike last time." The darkness seemed to be attracted to her, and I could hardly see her face. "Tell your friends to head back to the compound. We need to exchange words."

Liam stepped in front of me. "We won't let you hurt her."

She sighed. "Foolish boy, if I wanted to hurt her, I would have already done so."

Ayre stepped up next to Liam and formed a blockade between Sariah and me. "You can't have her."

I could see a smile stretching across Sariah's face. It practically glowed in the dark. "Good thing I do what I want." She snapped her fingers, and we were alone. I looked around frantically for my best friend. She was gone.

"What do you want and what did you do to them?"

"Your little friends are safe back at home, where they belong. The streets of New Orleans are not safe, or did you forget about the curfew?" Sariah cocked her head. I wished I could see her face, but the shadows were concealed her.

"We have things we need to do. Like I don't

know, get Sterling back." I crossed my arms over my chest.

"You don't have to hate me." She almost sounded hurt.

"What am I supposed to do?" I asked. I looked down at the pavement and avoided looking in her direction this time.

"I wish I had the answer to that. Don't you want to know what happened?" She now sounded defeated, and I knew this conversation would go nowhere, but I was a tad curious.

"I'm sure you're going to tell me anyway."

"Walk with me." She held her hand out, but I didn't take it. I met her halfway and kept up with her pace. "I fell in love with your father when I was a little girl."

I didn't know if I wanted her to go on, but she did.

"I followed him around everywhere, he hated it, but eventually when we were grown, I grew on him." She chuckled. "We didn't do things the traditional way. Our union was not blessed by the Council and my mother, your grandmother, swore it was why we were cursed with twins. Twins were something that had never happened before, and it baffled the covens. Especially twins to the High

Priestess. I, however, didn't think either of you was a curse and I love you both very much, but the coven didn't. I watched as your brother got sick and his magic didn't manifest at all. Over the course of two years, I beamed with joy as you flourished in your magic and anything else you touched. Your brother was the opposite, and I began to grow afraid."

I avoided looking in her direction. I could hear the emotion breaking up her words and tearing her apart. I should have stopped the story while I had a chance.

She continued, "Your father was in denial from the beginning and refused to see anything wrong with his son. I didn't know how to save my child and my marriage. That's another story for another day, but while he pushed it all under the rug, I was in the libraries searching for something to save him. I'm sure you know what happened next."

I could almost hear it. I shook my head. I wasn't ready for the memory, but it came anyway.

"Please, please forgive me." My mother wept at my feet, but I didn't know why she was crying. My little hand reached out and brushed her hair from her face. Her lavender eyes looked up and pleaded with me. "I love you both too much, I can't lose y'all."

I staggered backward and almost fell. "I'm not ready for this."

"You have to be." When I looked up at my mother's face, I lost my footing. The shadows had been hiding her for a reason. Black veins had made their way down her face and the once beautiful woman she had been was now gone. I crab-walked backward until I hit the curb and I fell down to the cobblestones beneath me. "I am not telling you these things to hurt you. I am telling you these things to prepare you for when you see him, you will remember, and it will rip you apart. You will hesitate, and you will die."

"My father?" I still wasn't catching on.

"No, your brother." She closed her eyes, and I watched as tears made streams down her blackened cheeks.

"I thought he was dead, that you killed him."

"I should have." When Sariah opened her eyes, it was like her soul was gone.

"I don't understand."

"No more interruptions." She commanded, no more softness in her voice. "I found dark magic, and I thought it was the only thing that could save him. Unfortunately, I needed both of you for the ritual to work. I don't know if you ever knew, but the scar on your hip, it was from that night."

I hadn't thought much about it. I didn't remember how I got it, so I had always thought the thick, deep scarring there was something that happened when I was a baby. I didn't know why I hadn't thought of it when I had ended up here. I lifted up my shirt and touched the tender skin there. A long silver scar stretched from under my belly button right above my pants to almost my back. Chills covered my entire body.

"I am not proud of what I am about to tell you, but you have to know." She tried to touch my hand, and I moved just out of her grasp. "I sliced you and your brother there, but something happened, something went wrong. The dark magic and the essence, I don't know. All I know is that I lost everything that night."

"And yet, here you are, here you are conspiring against me and the coven and continuing to hurt everyone around you!" I shouted at her. People turned to look at us on the now crowded streets, but they quickly looked away when they spotted Sariah's face.

"Do you honestly think this is what I want to

do?" She touched her face with both hands and bared her teeth at me.

"Why else would you be doing it?" I scowled at her.

"I have no choice. Dark magic comes with a price, a price that can never and will never be paid in full. Learn that now so you don't hurt and regret like I do. I just couldn't stand to see my son die and not do anything to save him. Unfortunately, I lost you both in the process. I know that the essence protected you and hid you and your memories."

"I guess that makes sense." I paused and looked at her. The woman that was my mother, but not the woman that was showing up in my memories that were coming forth now. I stared at the stranger, the shell of a woman that I could have known, I could have loved. "I feel like there is a 'but' coming."

"There is." She squeezed her eyes closed. "I wanted revenge. I wanted revenge against the coven that had forced me to go to extremes. I wanted to crush everything in my anger, and then I felt you dying. I felt your soul leave New Orleans and I had no time to think. I couldn't lose you again. So I gave it all up. Not that your dragon gave me much say in the matter, but I gave up the powers to save you."

I felt a nagging at my brain, something wasn't

adding up, and I was afraid to ask. I skipped around the subject instead. "What happened to my dad?"

"He went looking for you, not believing that you were dead," Sariah said, softly.

"Where is he now?"

"He's waiting for the right time, I would imagine. I have no doubt the Council has notified him of your return." There was something else. I could feel it.

"And why would they do that?" I asked, unsure of myself.

"Because he is a member of the Council." *There is was.*

"All Council members must be present when they are called forth, right?" I asked, I was somewhere far away in my mind. I couldn't seem to stop the spinning going on in my head.

"Yes," she said it like she knew.

"Then, then I have already met my father, but I just have to figure out who he is."

Sariah remained quiet.

"Why didn't anyone tell me?" I asked her, growing impatient.

"What would you have them tell you? They have to respect his wishes, they can't just out him, especially if he doesn't want to be outed." She shook her head and took a deep breath.

"How did you know?"

"I figured there would be a calling of the Council after the rougarou attack. I just didn't know if they would allow you to be present or not." She reached her hand out as if she was going to touch me, then she let it drop, and her shoulders slumped.

"The rougarours weren't your doing were they?" I asked, but I felt like I already knew the answer.

"No, they weren't."

"But you know who created them," I said.

She tilted her head back and forth, considering her answer. "Yes, and no."

"I hate half ass answers." My temper was starting to flare up. More secrets were being kept from me and now just another roadblock. I could have screamed, and I would have if we were surrounded by a bunch of humans.

She actually had the audacity to smile. "You remind me of your father. You have his temperament."

"Tell me who killed me." I was all about finding everything out tonight. I didn't know how much time I had left with the woman that birthed me, but

I was going to make it count. I had no doubt that Jonathan had already sent out the cavalry with their pitchforks and torches, ready to burn the witch.

"You aren't ready." She looked defeated.

"Tell me who killed me." I faced her head on. I needed to know.

"I can't Frey," The nickname surged something within me, and I had to blink away tears. "It will destroy you."

Tears blurred my vision. "Tell me." My voice broke, but I didn't back down.

"Your brother."

CHAPTER TWENTY

W hen I woke up, Shay was gone. I didn't plan on searching her out, but I needed to get out of this bedroom. The little dragon that was disguised as a cat followed me right out of the room and down the stairs. The stairs lead directly to the blood bar that was now empty beside a black haired beauty sitting on a barstool.

"It's a little early, don't you think?" I asked, sitting on the bar stool next to the Snow White.

"You snore," Shay muttered as she knocked back the rest of her amber colored drink.

"I don't doubt it."

"You look weird in jeans." She replied.

"Is it insult Sterling day?" I asked.

"I'm not in the mood for your cheery attitude."

"I'm going to be honest, I have never been told that before." The cat curled around my feet and went to sleep, though every few seconds she would peek an eye open. I caught on that she was not okay with our current residence, and I didn't blame her. "Where is everyone?"

She shrugged and leaned over the bar. Her skirt lifted up, and I could see everything, I avoided the eyeful as much as I could and looked at her hands instead. She had a bottle of vodka clutched tightly as she threw herself back down and took a swig from the bottle.

"Probably not very sanitary," I muttered. "And you're probably not going to be feeling too hot pretty soon, depending on how long you have been down here."

"One: the alcohol here is to keep up appearances if mortals come in, which they usually don't. Two: I have done everything in existence to get high, trust me when I say, alcohol does nothing to me or my magi anymore." She brushed her hair away from her ear, and I noticed she had a helix piercing with a big gem.

"I have never seen a magi as an earring," I admitted.

"I guess I'm rare." She rolled her eyes and knocked back some more clear alcohol.

"No doubt about that," I muttered.

She shrugged while drinking from the bottle again. "I haven't seen anyone since I woke up hours ago."

Like we had summoned him, the door burst open, and light streamed brightly into the bar. Cullen was wearing biker boots, tight black leather pants, and no shirt. He had tattoos covering his pale skin, and his hair was brushed back from his face.

"Good morning family!" He beamed. "I see we are getting a healthy start to our day!"

We didn't say anything.

"So upbeat and chipper this morning," Cullen said, sarcastically. "Sterling, I would like a word, please and thank you."

He motioned me forward with a jeweled finger. My familiar stayed quick on my heels as we entered another room. "I want you to tell me about my sister. I hear you are quite the expert."

I laughed. "I don't know about that."

"Humor me." He opened the door and in the middle of the room was a formal dining table with five chairs on either side of it. "I have heard you have spent much time with her."

"On and off. I have spent more time with Shay."
I bated him, trying to see if I could get a reaction.

He showed no type of emotion. "Interesting.
She will be a distraction then?"

I shook my head. "I have my sights exactly
where I need them."

One side of his mouth quirked up before he
turned away from me and sat in one of the chairs at
the end of the room. I touched the velvet on the
one across from him before I took a seat myself.
"Would you call that a challenge?"

"Not entirely. You interest me."

Both sides of his mouth quirked up, and his
dead eyes watched me head on. "Are you trying to
come onto me?" He leaned forward.

It was my turn to smirk at him. "Not at all."

Cullen pouted and sat back in his chair. "Then
what is it?"

"Your power intrigues me. I remember you as a
child, and you were nothing like you are now. I
would be lying if I said I wasn't curious." I crossed
my arms over my chest and leaned back in my chair
too. Might as well get comfortable.

"My mother did this to me." He frowned. "I
should be thanking her, but yet, where is she?

Obsessing over my dear, twin sister just like everyone else."

Something about the way he said that made me nervous for Freya, but I didn't let it show on my face. "What do you mean?"

His lip twitched up in a scowl. "Freya should be dead. The only reason she lives is because of Mother. When I sent my Rou out there to make sure the job had been completed, I found him injured and not by the powers of a wee little-lost witch. His injuries were extensive you see, the power from her blow had shot straight through him. This alarmed me and rightfully so, how would my sweet sister do such damage? Then I find out that she has grown into her ancestral, God-given powers? Sounds a little fishy, so I sent another Rou out, and to my surprise, a little bird came back to report something interesting." He stopped talking and had a faraway look on his face.

"And what was that?" I asked.

"She had the connection with her people. She felt the soul lost and did what a High Priestess does when they lose one of their own. No training, she just knew what to do." Cullen wrapped a piece of hair around his finger and watched me. "Mother saved her precious protege again and left me for ruin."

"She warned me about you." I considered my words carefully, like when I spoke to my father. "Told me that there was a storm brewin', so to speak."

Cullen smiled and bore his teeth. "She ain't wrong. There is a storm a-brewin', Sterling and you'll be on the winner's side." He stood up and clapped me on the back. He didn't look back as he left the room and all I could do was sit there and watch him go.

CHAPTER TWENTY-ONE

FREYA

Just like I had predicted, Jonathan's crew came barreling through the Quarter with their magic blazing and ready. He had cut our conversation short, and it irked me beyond belief. Sariah had just dropped a bomb on me, and there was no way for me to ask any more questions or get any kind of closure. He had escorted me back to the compound like a punished child.

But this wasn't over, it was far from it. I was the High Priestess here. I marched my way to the study and threw the doors open, but the scene before me had me frozen in the doorway. Jonathan was sitting at the desk, and a man was leaning against the other side of it with his arms wide. He was literally shouting in Jonathan's face. "She deserves to know!"

They hadn't noticed my intrusion, so I took the moment to observe the man with his back to me. It was the same man from the Council meeting, the one that had worn a tank top and ripped jeans and tattoos covering his arms. He was wearing something similar to the meeting a few nights prior. His dirty blonde hair was braided across the top of his head then tied off in a high knot. His arms had rippling muscles, and I was pretty sure if I didn't stop staring, I would be caught. I cleared my throat ready to rip Jonathan and The Council member a new one when the stranger turned around. There was something familiar about him that I had realized before. I took a step back and shook my head. The memories came quickly and had me gasping through tears.

The man before me partially resembled the man in my mind. The man in front of me was indeed a stranger.

"Freya." His voice held a tenderness, and his face had hardened through the years. There were new wrinkles and a stubble on his face that he had kept cleanly shaven when I was a child. I didn't know why I hadn't recognized him before. I didn't understand why all of this had to happen to me now.

I shook my head. Jonathan stood up, and my anger came back blazing hot. I pointed my finger at him. "Don't you ever treat me like a child again."

"Don't you ever do something like that again!" he retorted.

"Last time I checked I was the High Priestess, not you!"

"Last time I checked we had both agreed on a curfew for the coven!" he shouted.

"I do not need your permission!" I knew I sounded spoiled, but I was on a roll, and I didn't plan on stopping. "I didn't ask for any of this and dammit, if my mother needs to speak with me, we will speak! She saved my life!"

"She did more than just save your life! She has caused you so many problems!" Jonathan pinched the bridge of his nose. "You worried me."

"I was going to come back." I looked to the floor, unsure of myself.

"How was I supposed to know that? You have disappeared a lot lately." He threw his hands up in agitation.

"You don't need to worry about me," I whispered.

"And why not?" Jonathan yelled.

"You're not my father, and you've kept enough from me as it is." I bit my lip to keep myself from crying. Dammit, I would not cry.

"That was my fault." The man said.

A tear spilled over, and I cursed myself. This was not the time for that nonsense. I shook my head at him, it wasn't the time for his nonsense either.

"Let me explain." The man held his large hands up in surrender. I closed my eyes, I didn't know what to do. "Your mother came back into your life, the coven, a dragon familiar, The Mirror Realm. How was I supposed to compete with any of that? How was I supposed to just drop in and say 'Hey Kiddo' like no time had passed, like you remembered me when I knew damn well that you didn't."

I swallowed thickly and couldn't speak. I just let him continue while I watched Jonathan retreat out the corner of my eye. I wanted him to know this wasn't over, but I didn't have the guts to start speaking again. I was afraid I would betray myself with my stupid tears.

"I waited for the right moment, but I guess there is no right moment." He smiled, and it was like looking in the mirror. I had his smile, I could see it clear as day. I wanted to smile with him, but the stubbornness inside of me made me bite my lip and stop with all this mushy crap.

"Sariah told me about you last night." It was the only thing I could say. His face fell. "Nothing bad. I didn't know you were alive."

He looked at the books on the wall like they would give him some type of wisdom to get through this. "I didn't know you were alive either. I searched for you, all over the world. Then one day I had to stop, my magi was restless, and I was weak." He held up his arm and on his wrist was a magi similar to mine, but very different. The stone was the color mine had been, garnet and the jewelry that held in place was corded metal knotting and unknotting all around the beautiful gem.

I held my arm up to show him mine. I pushed my sleeve away from it, and his eyes had so much pride in them, another tear slipped down my cheek. "My stone was the same color. It changed when I became High Priestess."

"Your mother's did the same thing, but she didn't have a dragon, so it just turned lighter, instead of a different color altogether." He shrugged and shook his head. "You look just like her."

I didn't want to hear it. My mind and emotions

could only take so much. I wanted to know him though, and I knew that time was always limited. Someone would need me, or maybe Sterling would come back. I needed to do what I could now. "Where did you get your tattoos?"

He smiled and looked down at them lovingly. "When I was looking for you, I came across the Scandinavian coven. These are runes from their gods and their religion. I fell in love with their culture and stayed awhile." It explained the way his voice tilted and not in a southern way anymore. It also explained the hair. "I learned a lot about myself there. Maybe one day you will come visit with me, and maybe we could move my stuff back here. I do miss the food." He winked, and I didn't blame him. The food here was like nowhere else in the world.

"Did you know that my brother killed me?" As much as I didn't want to get into emotional stuff, here I was poking the bear.

His eyes turned cold. "No. Jonathan did what he could to leave that part out."

"Jonathan doesn't know who did it. He just knew that I died." I whispered and then shuddered. It was like I wasn't even talking about myself anymore.

"Cullen is the reason you are High Priestess then?"

At the mention of his name, I had a flash of a boy running with me with long red hair and a smile bigger than his face. We were holding hands, our freckles matching and our pale skin glowing. I blinked, and the memory was gone.

Cullen. Cullen and Freya.

Pain sliced through my heart. My entire life I had dreamed of a family, and here it was. Here it was, giving me everything and taking it all away. I swallowed again, and I sniffled. I wiped at my face and tried my hardest to keep it together. My brother. My own twin had killed me. What kind of twisted fate was this? What had I done to deserve such a thing?

The door to the study opened, and Cassie came to a screeching halt. "Tavin." She gasped. She shook her head. "I didn't know you were here."

"It's okay, Cassie, no need to get emotional on me." But his voice was thick with emotion too.

"It's just been so long." She looked between us and the waterworks came. Leave it to Cassie to fall apart first. I would never admit that I had been the first to shed a tear, but Cassie would take one for the team.

"I think I am back for good," Tavin said. "Freya, you think that would all right? I promise to be good."

"Only if you bring me to Scandinavia when all of this is over," I said, full of sass.

"I wouldn't have it any other way." He grasped my shoulder and looked into my eyes. Whatever he saw there had a smile touching his lips as he pulled me forward into the best hug I had ever had, except maybe Sterling's. Those were pretty great, but I probably wouldn't ever tell him that. He didn't need any more confidence.

CHAPTER TWENTY-TWO

STERLING

S hay gave me a funny look as I straightened the tie on my suit.

"What's wrong?" I asked.

"You don't feel weird going back?" She turned away from me and sat on the bed. She put her silver heels beside her and leaned forward. Her hair fanned forward and hid her face.

"We aren't going back," I said, dusting off my pants. Cat hair was the worst.

"We are though, in a way."

"It's a masquerade, I doubt anyone will pay us any attention," I replied. I grabbed the gel from the table and scowled. A man who didn't fix his hair had bought this. Cullen didn't know a thing about the good stuff, but it would do. I scooped out a healthy amount and slicked my hair back. I didn't typically fashion my hair this way, and that's why I was doing it. I didn't want to be recognizable. I wanted to get the job done and get back here before anything else happened.

"*I'm going with you.*" The voice in my head had me jump and let out a squeak. The dragon sat at my feet looking up at me with unblinking eyes.

"I'm going to take it that we are bonded now," I said to her, paying no attention to Shay.

"*Not fully, but it'll be soon. That's why I can't leave you.*"

"Are you sure you aren't interested in seeing a certain dragon while we are there?"

"*I am not following.*"

"Vailen, the last dragon. He will probably be there."

The cat disguise started to go in and out, and I didn't know if it was because my magic was faulty or because she was having a hard time in her skin.

"*Vailen? He is here?*" Her voice was different and emotional in my mind.

"Oh good, you do know him." I wiped my hands on a towel. "You have to stay away from him tonight. He was overly protective of your egg, and the Priestess can't know I'm there. In fact, no one can so if you are going to accompany me, you have to be careful, and you have to stay in this form."

"*I have never liked taking orders, especially from witches.*" She stretched forward and her tail curled in the air.

"This is to keep us both safe. Stop being sassy. I thought I had escaped that when I came here." As soon as the words left my mouth, I found myself missing Freya. I had escaped her sassiness, but I would be a liar to say that I hadn't enjoyed it.

She rolled her blue feline eyes and stalked away.

Shay interrupted the quiet with a shocked voice. "You have bonded with her then?"

I shrugged my shoulders. "I would imagine so."

"What's her name?" I hadn't thought to even ask.

"*Callia,*" She answered in my mind.

I repeated it to Shay. Shay's eyes narrowed. "I fear there are more dragons out there."

I stopped messing with my suit and Callia jumped onto the bed beside her. "What do you mean?"

"I mean the dragon that Cullen wanted, it wasn't a female, and it certainly wasn't Callia." She gave me a worried glance. Her eyes held fear.

"Do you know what the name of the dragon

was, Shay?" I asked, hesitantly. I could see Callia's stance changing. She was tensing up, almost like she was preparing for a fight.

"He wanted Drake." Shay was pinned against the bed in seconds. Callia was no longer a little cat, but now a huge, fierce dragon holding the woman down. Smoke was billowing from her nostrils. Shay gave me a look of acceptance like she wanted to die.

"Callia, she is not the one you want. You know this. Breathe through your rage, breathe through the pain. Tell me who Drake is." Images flashed through my mind like a movie. A little red dragon that looked like Vailen falling in the snow, he tried to stand up, but his wings were full of slush, and he toppled forward.

"*Drake is my son.*" Pain pierced through me like bullets. "*My only son.*"

FREYA

"YOU'RE GOING to hate me for this." I crossed my arms over my chest. Vailen kept his eyes closed. "Stop ignoring me."

He blinked one eye open and watched me.

"You can't come tonight," I said as I reached my hand deep into the bag on my bed. I imagined a deep blue dress with long sleeves and a high neckline, and backless. It was still getting chilly in New Orleans, and the rain had been non-stop. I would have been silly to wear anything else.

"*You don't need to g o alone.*"

"I won't be alone, Vailen. My father is escorting me." The dress appeared in my hand, the soft material tickling my fingers. I sent a silent thank you to Wyna and stripped down. I pulled the billowing dress down over my head and let it slide into place.

"*What if he can't see the danger that I can from the sky?*" Vailen had his eyes closed again.

"Are you really *that* worried about it?" I asked as I ran my hands down the dress, making sure it fit snug to my body. I turned around and gazed at my pale back in the mirror. Freckles marked across my shoulders and down my spine like little constellations. My scar peaked out just barely.

"*Yes, I sense trouble in the air.*" His tone left no room for argument. As much as I loved to argue, I would get nowhere with the beast tonight. He was in a mood.

"Fine, but you have to remain in the sky or on

top of the building. No funny business." I pointed at him like I was scolding a child. He rolled his eyes at me.

"You have my word."

I twisted my hair up and then untwisted it, unsure of myself and my hair fixing skills. I wished Ayre was here, but she seemed more and more MIA lately. Liam stole most of her time away. I was a little jealous, especially since the one that filled those gaps had purposefully left me.

A knock at the door had my dropping my hair. It fell over my shoulders in helpless piles. I sighed and yanked the door open.

Tavin took up the space comfortably. He looked handsome in a suit, and I wondered why he didn't dress nicer more often until he started to pull at the collar, and I understood. Comfort was important. On either side of his face, he had braids pulling back the rest of his hair. It kept it free from his face, and he looked like a Viking king made over.

"You look radiant, daughter. But your face tells me you are troubled, what's the matter?" He closed the door behind him and eyed the sleeping beast on my bed. For dramatic effect, Vailen let smoke rise from his nostrils. I let out an exasperated sigh.

"Nothing, just trying to figure out what to do

with all of this." I made crazy motions around my head and threw myself down next to Vailen. Tavin clasped his hands in front of him and smiled.

"It's strange to see you so casual with a monster."

Vailen blinked his eyes open and started to rise to the challenge. "Down boy." I giggled.

Vailen slinked from the bed and walked around my father, sizing him up as he grew bigger. He went from the size of a house cat to the size of a lion rather quickly. Tavin wasn't bothered by it and let Vailen do his surveying before Vailen got bored and left us alone completely.

"He's temperamental," I explained.

"I've heard the same about you." He let out a hearty laugh.

"Touché."

"Sit up, let me help you." He motioned for me to come closer to him until I was perched on the edge of the bed. His fingers worked magic in my hair, and when I looked in the mirror, I looked like a princess. It was expertly braided back up and away from my face.

"Simply gorgeous." I smiled at him in the mirror as he put his hands on my shoulders. "I do have to say, it is odd."

I turned around and frowned up at him. "What?"

"Seeing you so grown up and the back of this dress doesn't help." He chuckled. I raised an eyebrow. "Don't worry, I have nothing to say. You are a grown woman, and you make your own decisions. I'm also a little thankful that the man that has caught your eye won't be there tonight. I would probably be a little protective then."

I tried to not let my disappointment show, but it was too late. Tavin put his finger under my chin and lifted my face so I would look at him. "If he's worth it, he will be there."

Tavin held my hand as we approached the building. The Christmas lights were gorgeous and added the right effect to the ambiance. I pulled my dress from my feet before we started up the stairs. My heart was beating out of my chest, and I was happy to be grasping my father's hand. He kept me tethered in place. I could hear Vailen's wings from above. He had insisted again, so I didn't argue. He always had his reason, and he would either be here, and I know it, or he would be here, and I would know it, but not agree with it. Vailen did what he wanted until I commanded him, and I hated doing that, so he did his own thing.

Tavin pushed the double doors open in front of me, and the crowd turned to gaze upon me. I swallowed hard and stopped walking. Tavin's rough hand pressed into my back and encouraged me forward. Everyone in the room was wearing a mask.

Every mask was just as different and significant as the next. I had chosen not to wear one and Tavin had a small black one that just wrapped around his eyes. There was a stage on the opposite side of the room, and I could see Cassie and Jonathan speaking to someone. I looked at every face as I made my way to the stage, hoping that I would see familiar features. It was no use, all the men wore outlandish masks, and every single one of them were strangers.

People reached out and touched me as I walked by, they grabbed my hands, whispered prayers and just wanted a glimpse at their High Priestess. I turned to Tavin, and he was at my ear already. "They do it as a sign of respect, and love. They also hope that good fortune will befall them. They are here for *you*."

I swallowed down my nerves and reached out to grasp hands as I went. Some were perplexed and stepped away from me. Others fell at my feet as I went by. I pulled them up and squeezed their hands tenderly. I wasn't a god. I was just a girl.

When I made it to the raised platform, Tavin held my hand as I made my way up the steps. He stayed below and crossed his arms over his chest. When I met Cassie and Jonathan, the person they had been talking to turned around.

Agata.

She gave me a hug and whispered, "It is my pleasure to serve you, my lady. This night is about you. Enjoy."

She left the stage and Jonathan came forward. He grasped my hand in his. He wore a dark gray suit and a phantom mask that covered half of his face. Cassie wore an elaborate ball gown with her hair in little pin curls. She didn't wear a mask, but she was breathtaking.

"Enjoy the night, we will do all the talking and all the introductions," Cassie said as she grasped my hands in hers. "You deserve to enjoy your people and your city."

CHAPTER TWENTY-THREE

STERLING

My heart stopped when she walked in. She looked like a goddess. I couldn't take my eyes off her, no matter how many times Shay cleared her throat. When I finally noticed the man on her arm the room went a little red. I had no reason to be jealous, but I would be a liar if I said I wasn't. I had never met the man before, though something about him was familiar and though I hadn't been gone very long; she had every right to move on or to find someone new. If anything but to keep appearances, I understood.

I watched her march up the steps, and my parents greet her fondly. When she turned away from me, my mouth dropped open. Her entire back was exposed, and even though she should have been cold, I could tell she wasn't. Her bodyguard's eyes scanned the room and landed on me. His lips pressed together, and his eyes narrowed behind his black mask. I had been caught. I had thought my mask had been disguise enough.

I was wrong. He observed me, not taking his eyes off of me once. They flicked once toward Shay, and that was for a faint moment. He took his coat off and pushed his sleeves up, readying himself for a fight. His arms were marked up to the elbows in tattoos, and I had no doubts that they went higher. Where had they found this man? His eyes were bright purple, but he seemed to like physical defense more than the magical kind, judging by the scarring near his neck and on his hands.

Shay grabbed my hand, and I looked down in shock. I looked up at her face, and she gave me a warning, shaking her head. When I looked back at the stage, the man was gone. I scowled at Shay but didn't give her the full effect because the man was standing behind Shay.

His stare was predatory. This wasn't good at all. I hadn't even worn a suit that my mother would recognize. He twitched his head to the left toward a door. There weren't many people in between us and I knew I could make it out, either by running or using magic. But I had a feeling this wasn't the time to make my getaway. He pulled me into a butler's closet and closed the door behind us, leaning against it. I had wished I had seen Shay's face as we made our way, but I was trying to not look suspicious, and I didn't want Freya to recognize me.

"So, *you're* Sterling." His voice was confusing. It had all sorts of different accents mixed in it. "I've heard a lot about you." He crossed his arms over his chest, the lighting was dull, so I wasn't able to get a good look at him still.

"Warnings maybe?"

His lips twitched into an amused smile. "I would hope not."

I crossed my arms over my chest. "Why not?"

"Would you want the father of your love interest to know all of your misconduct?"

What the? I cocked my head at him and frowned. He removed his mask, and there was something familiar about the shape of his eyes and the setting of his nose. I swallowed nervously.

"It's nice to see you again Sterling Masters, you probably don't remember me. I left after the disappearance of my twins and didn't come back until recently. My daughter asked me to stay, and quite frankly, I wouldn't tell a High Priestess no. Would you?" His amused smile was back, and I could feel my heart hit my stomach.

"I guess we started this a bit wrong." I held my hand out to shake his and tried to calm my nerves.

"You don't want Freya to know you're here or your parents I would presume?" He shook my hand and went back to his spot on the door.

"No, I would like to keep my dealings a secret for now," I said, trying to calm my heart and my stomach. First impressions were everything, and I had just seriously botched this up.

"As long as you aren't doin' her dirty, I don't care what you do. You treat her right, and you are okay with me." He narrowed his eyes at me, put his mask back on and pulled the door open. He was gone within seconds, and I was left standing there feeling like I was going to be sick. He hadn't even told me his name. I leaned over and put both of my hands on my knees and tried to breathe.

The door opened up, and I was like a soldier, I went up ramrod straight like nothing had been ailing me. When I saw it was Shay, I relaxed a little bit, but she wasn't dumb.

"What just happened in here?" she asked, suspiciously.

I wiped my brow. "I met Freya's father."

Her eyes got wide. "What do you mean by that? That man is her father?"

I nodded my head.

She immediately started to look me over for injuries. "Did he hurt you?"

"I almost wish he would have. The worst first impression I've ever had."

Shay cocked an eyebrow and laughed. "Really because rumor around the compound was that Freya's was even worse."

I had almost forgotten about that. I could feel myself starting to blush, and I didn't usually do that. "Yeah, that wasn't my finest moment." I thought for a minute before I continued on. "But actually, there weren't many good moments until she came back from The Mirror Realm."

"I heard that too." She patted me on the shoulder. "Don't beat yourself up. We all have things that we wish we could change, might as well work to be better while we can."

I frowned. "You are planning something." I didn't need to ask. I could feel the change in her. Her words just confirmed it.

"I can't tell you what I have to do." She looked at the floor, her hair falling forward. "You can't know because you can't be involved."

I grabbed her face in my hands and guided her to look into my eyes. "I want to help you."

Her eyes filled with tears, but she blinked them back. She smiled and shook her head. "There are no survivors where I am going."

She pulled her face from my hands and dashed from the room.

Alone again. It seemed to be what the universe and essence preferred for me as of late.

CHAPTER TWENTY-FOUR

FREYA

I watched Tavin return just as quickly as he had left. He wore an amused expression on his face, and I wondered what kind of trouble he had found. He put his warm hand on the small of my back and guided me to the refreshments table.

"What's so funny?" I asked, not letting him distract me with the fancy food put out in front of us.

"Nothing, Daughter."

I rolled my eyes. "I would imagine that I am a lot like you, and if that is the case, then you probably already know that I don't like to be told no." I crossed my arms over my chest and glared at him.

He smiled widely. "It seems that people think I am your date."

I grimaced at him. "Is that what you were doing? Making people aware that you are the father of The High Priestess and not a date?"

"I am very much your date." The corners of his mouth pulled down. "In a *very* platonic way."

"Okay, then what was the disappearing about?" I asked, piling food up on a plate. "Do you have a very *non*-platonic date hiding somewhere?"

Tavin gave out a hearty laugh and shook his head, following me down the table. "I don't think he would appreciate that statement."

I was about to take a bite out of a boudin ball and stopped. "*Oh my gosh,* are you gay?" I whispered.

He just laughed harder.

"I am not judging you. I mean it would explain why you didn't remarry or come back for mom when she escaped." I hurried to get all my words out, though I was struggling to do so. My mind was going 90 to nothing.

He sobered up quick at the words of Sariah. "I no longer have business with that woman, Freya. Understand that over anything else. Your mother changed when your brother was sick. It twisted her and made her into a monster."

I blinked my eyes and tried to keep up with the emotional change. I quickly scarfed down the boudin ball, not enjoying it one bit and looked around the room for a place to sit. At least I could try to enjoy the rest. Jambalaya, meat pies, sausage and what seemed to be fried alligator lay on the crystal plate between my hands. Tavin grabbed the plate and motioned for me to get us drinks from a server walking around the room. He made his way toward the stage. There was a table set up with the Masters, Agata and a few others I didn't recognize. I grabbed two flutes of Champagne when a man passed in front of me.

I opened my mouth to call after him, then closed it. My mind had to be playing tricks on me. I blinked and tried to follow him with my eyes through the crowd. He disappeared before I could get my wits about me.

I shook my head. I was being silly. There were probably many different men that had a similar build to him, with the same hair cut and hair color. I just missed him too much, and it was starting to affect me.

When I sat down, Tavin was watching me carefully. "Are you all right?"

I smiled at him reassuringly. "Yes, I just thought I saw someone I knew." My eyes involuntarily looked for him again in the crowd, but he was long gone, whoever he was.

Tavin frowned as he ate his food, but he didn't say anything else. My thoughts of Sterling drowned out Jonathan's words on the stage, and as people started to mill toward me, I regretted being lost in my thoughts. Tavin stood up from the table to greet people as they came up, many of the introductions were lost on me, and I just smiled and pretended like I would remember any of it.

Finally, all the faces were gone, and I was able to eat in peace.

Ayre sat beside me, and Liam was on the other side of her. "This place is boring," she whispered. "Zero stars, do not recommend."

I rolled my eyes. "What do you want it to be? A huge dance party?"

She gave me a tight-lipped, sarcastic smile. "Well, yeah. Next party the coven throws, you have to appoint me as *the* party planner."

"Well, I think your mom might be upset about that," I said, in-between bites of the fried meat, it was definitely alligator. It was perfection, and I was without a doubt going to go back for seconds.

"Well, I think someone new needs to be in charge." She leaned back in her chair and pouted. Liam rolled his eyes behind her like he didn't agree at all.

I was about to say something when Cassie put her hand on my arm and drew my attention her way. She was smiling at the woman sitting catty-corner to me. "This is Ada. She is the queen of the Vampires in the Quarter."

The food in my mouth turned to ashes. I thought this was a coven party, but then I remembered Agata and could see her out of the corner of my eye at the other end of the table.

"It's nice to see a new *young* face at the head of the New Orleans Coven." She gave me a toothy grin that showed her elongated canines. I glanced at Tavin, and he nodded his head forward like I could trust her.

"Thank you," I didn't know how to speak to these people, but I figured confidence was the key. I had power unimaginable, and I wanted to be at the top of the food chain. "This is a big change to what I am used to, but I am confident that I can do what it takes to make the coven the best it has ever been."

"Big words from a new little witch." A dark man seated next to her muttered.

I narrowed my eyes, and out the corner of my eye, I watched Tavin clench his fist. "I have confidence in myself, and I don't care if you have it. I will do whatever it takes to prove all of you, *naysayers*, wrong."

He lifted his head up and licked his top lip. His dark hair was cropped short, and he was grinning at me. "You got fire, kid."

I cocked my head and snarled. "I know how to use it too."

"Oh yeah?" He was bating me, I could feel it, but I was too far into my temper to care.

"Yeah, you heard of *my* dragon, right?" I kept a straight face, waiting for the right moment. Tavin looked at me horrified like I should have kept my mouth closed. Like I should have kept my familiar home.

"The extinct creatures that your coven keeps name dropping to keep people afraid?" He gave me a predatory grin, his dark skin glowing in the dim lighting.

I gave one right back as I heard Vailen land behind me. Vailen was apart of me, and there was no reason to keep him hidden. He was just as much a part of the coven as I was and if someone wanted to come in and think they had power... I would show them power. I could feel his presense growing as he got bigger and towered over me.

The Vampire didn't even flinch. He narrowed his eyes. "Illusions do not scare me, little girl." I stood up slowly from my chair. I didn't know how illusions worked, but I was determined to scare him now. No one would call me *little* again. Being petite was one thing, but a child, I was not.

I ran my hands down Vailen's back as Tavin stood up and spoke for me, "The great thing about illusions is you can only make an illusion out of the size of what you are concealing. So, if this were an illusion, I would be afraid." The man watched my father warily. "Because she would have to have something monstrous to conceal to get an illusion this big or that much magic at her disposal and I have never heard of anything like that before."

Vailen's head was brushing the ceiling, and his tail was as long as the table now. The Vampire was making the wrong enemy. Smoke started to unfurl from Vailen's nostrils, and the Vampire's face grew worried. I focused solely on him, not concerned with anyone else in the room. Hotshot probably needed a shot now. I quirked an eyebrow at him.

Tavin continued on, "The great thing about an illusion, as I can see you realize is, they can't create what they don't have."

I shrugged my shoulders and smiled sweetly.

Vailen leaned forward and pressed his face against the Vampire's. I could see the man's Adam's apple bobbing and sweat beading on his forehead. Interesting, maybe he wasn't a vampire after all. Vailen spit out a small flame, and the man fell from his chair.

Vailen rolled his eyes and spoke in my mind. *"Are we done playing games with the mortal?"*

"You're human?" The words came from my mouth before I could stop them.

He narrowed his eyes at me. "No,"

There was something different about him, but I couldn't put my finger on it.

He waved his hands around casually, "The funny thing with these parties is, you have no security." Tavin's brow furrowed and started to make his way to my side. The mystery man continued on. "What's even funnier is, you don't recognize your own people."

His brown eyes were dark with hatred on me and then the emotion was gone. "You aren't one of us. I can feel it, barely there, but there is something that is keeping the link from flowing."

It was like a tug of magic under my skin. My magi didn't like what was happening because it started to warm on my wrist. Then the realization struck me, of course, the tether to the coven wouldn't be completed. "You're a half breed."

He raised his chin and looked me dead in the eyes. "You're a little quicker than your partners here."

Tavin slipped his hand in mine for support, or added strength. I didn't know what I was facing here. I hadn't learned about half breeds yet, and I wished terribly that Sterling was here.

"What you lack here in your little coven is diversity."

"What's your name?" I asked. I was done with the games he was playing, and people were starting to get curious. It didn't help that Vailen was towering over all of us.

"I am Stark. My last name doesn't matter, because you wouldn't know my father anyway. I am a bastard son, and I am a half breed." He sat back down at the table and continued to eat his food. The half breed part explained his eyes and why there was no magic there.

I tilted my head back and looked at Vailen. I needed answers.

He was hesitant, but he obliged. *"There aren't usually half breeds, they typically die in the womb. The essence has a way of taking care of them."*

I thought back to him. *"How do you know so much about this?"*

"I can read minds."

I threw my head back again and frowned at him.

"The witches are watching you, they are growing concerned."

I straightened up and gave all of the people at the table innocent looks. I yawned, but there was nothing fake about it. There was a clock hanging above the stage, and it was nearing midnight. I didn't want to be Cinderella and leave before the clock struck, but I was growing tired, and the politics were easily annoying. I let Jonathan and Cassie delegate, and I listened halfway to the conversation. As much as I wanted to be the full package of the Priestess roll, tonight was not the night for me to start. I didn't have the energy or the heart to hand it all, and the Masters had told me to enjoy my people, after all.

I kept my eyes on Stark, curious about what

brought him here tonight. My father had taken Ayre's spot at the table and was observing me, while he continued to eat. I stopped eating when everything had gone down, and I didn't care to continue.

I could feel Ayre's eyes on me from across the table, I didn't dare look in her direction. I could sense trouble and mischief coming off of her in waves. I really wished Sterling was here to balance her out, but poor Liam was stuck in her tornado. He looked like a lost puppy.

I looked Stark in the eyes. "Let's go talk."

My father stood up and put his hand on my arm. "I'll go with you."

I raised my eyebrows at him amused. "Remember that conversation we had before about how I'm like you?"

He pressed his lips together and ignored me.

"You'll do best if you let me do what I want," I said through a tight-lipped smile.

He released his hold on me begrudgingly and took a step back.

"Not only that, Vailen will be with me. He can and will protect me." I tried to give him a reassuring smile.

I flicked my head to the door, and Stark followed me out. Vailen stayed a good bit away from us. I shivered when the doors opened a breeze hit my back. I had managed to stay warm the entire night.

"Here let me help you." He held his hand out, and there was a flame dancing in the center of his palm. The chill went away and was replaced with me feeling cozy and comfortable. "What did you want to speak to me about?"

"I think you baited me on purpose," I said, carefully. "You wanted a private show with me."

When I looked at him out the corner of my eye, he had a guilty look on his face. "Yes, that might have been my end game. I have heard stories about your temperament, but also about how you are different."

I raised an eyebrow and guided him to the gardens. Many of the plants were now dead and not as pretty, but the grounds were well kept, and it gave me something to do. I was too antsy to sit still.

"I do have a temper," I said. I crossed my arms over my chest, feeling a tad defensive.

"I want change," he said.

Change is to come, no more stagnant coven. I tried to shake the whispers from my mind.

"Don't we all?" I asked. I turned back to him, and he was looking at me differently. Ugh, this stupid backless dress. I had thought it would be a good idea, but in fact, it was the opposite.

"I want to be apart of the coven."

"You will have to undergo a thorough truth serum. Do you think you can handle that?" I asked, wanting to give him the information The Hebert Pack should have provided me.

"Yes, my father kept me well informed on the things that surrounded the covens. He wanted this day for me." Stark bowed his head in reverence.

"How is this possible?" I asked, taking a seat on a concrete bench by a dry bird bath.

"I guess it shouldn't be, but I suppose we learned our lesson. My mother was ripped apart when she was giving birth to me."

I covered my mouth in horror. "That's terrible, I am so sorry."

"You have nothing to feel sorry for, you didn't grow up with either parent. I at least got my father while I could." He gave me a sad smile. He took a deep breath, and his broad shoulders seemed to get wider.

"What happened to him, if you don't mind me asking?"

He winced. "A new one came to this city. A few new ones came, and they brought destruction. I'm sure you know that" He bowed his head again. "My dad refused to bow to him, and he was killed. They thought of me as no threat, because my eyes do not resemble yours. I am sure you thought the same thing."

I shrugged a shoulder up. How was I supposed to just be afraid? Fear hadn't done me any favors.

"They let me live, but I am the only one left." Stark didn't sit down and continued to pace in front of me. "He is a monster."

"So, you came to warn me?" I asked.

He took a seat at my question and gave me a dazzling smile. "Yes, and I was wondering why your own father is your date."

I raised my eyebrows at him. I hadn't really noticed that he hadn't been wearing a mask like everyone else at the party, like he didn't care if someone knew his real face. Then it hit me, as his smile got bigger and his eyes softened, he wanted me to be able to see his face. His dark complexion was flawless, and his high cheekbones and sharp jawline were magazine worthy. He probably had no trouble with the ladies. Dark, thick eyelashes framed his big, deep brown eyes.

"You're too pretty to be here alone." He sounded out of breath.

"Does that line normally work for you?" I raised an eyebrow, mocking him. "I thought we were here for politics, not flirting."

"I wouldn't know, I have never used it before." He chuckled.

"I guess with a face like that, you wouldn't need to."

He leaned back and covered his heart with his hand, pretending to swoon. "Hmm, flirting."

I couldn't help the smile that overtook my face. Even though the first impression of this man hadn't been adept, he was making up for it.

"How did you know he was my father?" I asked, genuinely curious because men had been shooting Tavin daggers with their eyes all night. I hadn't missed the envious stares and glares around the room, from the women and men.

"For starters, he hasn't been handsy once. If you were my date, I wouldn't be able to keep my hands off of you, especially in this dress." He waggled his eyebrows at me. "Then when he stood up in your defense, I couldn't miss the resemblance."

"You're an observant one." I mocked.

He sobered up. "When you grow up where I did, it pays to be observant. Literally." His voice was sad, and I didn't know how to get the conversation back to happy.

"You grew up on the rough side of town," I said, dejected.

"Don't be a naive white girl." I looked at my silver shoes poking out from my dress. His tone was light, but it held more to it, and I didn't blame him, I was naive.

I looked into his eyes. "Educate me."

CHAPTER TWENTY-FIVE

STERLING

Shay had disappeared, and the dragon was out of the bag now. My eyes followed Freya as a man lead her out of the ballroom. There was no use in trying to pry. I had the information I needed for Cullen.

I clicked the dial on the side of my pocket watch and walked through to the blood bar. Cullen was nursing a beer like he could get drunk. "Your little girlfriend is upstairs."

I didn't reply to Cullen as I stalked up to the room we shared and pushed the door open. Callia was sleeping on the bed, and Shay was crying.

"What are you planning?" I stayed rooted to my spot at the door.

"I can't involve you in this. Go report back to

Cullen, and we will talk later." Shay pushed her hand forward, and a gust of wind shoved me from the room and down the stairs. My face slid across the tile on the bottom floor, and I felt myself brushing myself off and walking to Cullen like nothing had happened.

"She's a feisty one," Cullen muttered. "What do you have for me?"

"Your father is in town."

Cullen's eyes slowly connected with mine. "Well, this makes things interesting. What does he want?"

"I think he wants to protect Freya," I said, pretending to sound disgusted.

"Interesting. You didn't give yourself away, did you?" He sounded like he wouldn't believe me anyway.

"I did."

Cullen turned his whole body toward me, surprised. "I was waiting for you to lie to me."

"Your father came after me. We talked for a moment, and I pretended to be a lovesick puppy, caught in the middle of a war."

He knocked back a shot of amber liquid. "Aren't you?"

My lip twitched up. "Far from it."

"I don't know if I believe you, but you are on

the winner's side now, and that's all that matters." He folded his arms over his chest.

The air shimmered behind Cullen, and I knew what was going to happen next. I tried to keep my face emotionless and unseeing as Shay stepped through the air and stabbed Cullen in the back with a dagger.

He didn't even flinch. He turned around slowly and wrapped his fingers around her neck. This is what she meant. She knew she was going to die. Pain filled my chest, and I held my emotions in check. Cullen walked her across the room, her feet dangling from the air. He pressed her against the wall, and I went to stand. Maybe I could do something to stop him, to save her. Her eyes were red-rimmed and full of tears, she shook her head and whispered, "No!"

Cullen pressed her into the wall again with more force, and her head knocked against the sheetrock. My body fought with my emotions to go to her. She only looked at me while he screamed in her face and squeezed the life from her. I could feel myself losing the battle. I needed to stop him. The dagger through his back wasn't even stopping him. Was he even human?

He shook her like a rag doll and continued to

shove her into the wall. Shay didn't take her eyes off of me until eventually the light faded from them and her body went limp. Cullen laughed and spit on her before he threw her into a heap. Her vacant eyes stared at me, but there was no horror or grief there. Just peace. She had needed to rectify her sins, and this was the only way she thought she could do it. Cullen kicked her before he stormed from the building. Just as the door closed, he screamed my way, "Clean it up!"

The tears fell then, the ones I didn't know I had been holding in. I ran to her, my legs not fast enough for my body. I stumbled and tripped over myself until I was there. Right there next to her, closing her eyes and pulling her into my lap. He had strangled the life from her just like Freya. I pulled her higher in my arms and rocked her back and forth. I hadn't been able to save her.

I was a coward, and this was my fault. How had I let such a thing happen again and right in front of me? I sat there with her, not knowing what to do with her or myself.

I DIDN'T KNOW how much time had passed as I had sat there with her. The tears weren't stopping, and I could no longer see, but I stood up with her limp body anyway and clicked my magi. I walked through the air, right into the Paris Coven territory. I didn't know if I would make it out alive or if they would give me a truth serum to figure out what really happened. All I knew was that her family needed her and I could only do right by that.

A woman with gray hair was waiting for me. "Est-ce mon, Shay?"

"Yes," I croaked out. I didn't have the strength to speak French, even though it was second nature to me.

"What happened?" Her English was rough, but it was a pleasant sound.

"Axel did this to her." It was the name I knew they would recognize.

The woman fell to the ground and sobbed. A man rushed from the building on her side and grabbed her shaking shoulders. "What is happening?"

"I came to return her to her people," I said, numbly. The tears had stopped, and all that was left was a gaping hole. *This was my fault.* I wanted them to know, but the words wouldn't come out.

"I will get her mother." The woman said before she ran off. The man held his arms out to me, and I passed Shay's body to him. I scrubbed my hands down my face and tried my hardest to not fall apart again.

"You should go now. If you stay, it will be days before you can leave again." The man whispered to me.

"I don't plan on leaving, I want them to know what happened." My voice shook with raw emotions.

"They will perform magic on her body, and her magi will tell the story of her death to us, that is if he didn't take it."

I reached forward and brushed her long hair behind her ear and showed him her sparkling gem still there. He nodded his head and said, "Thank you, now go."

I looked over my shoulder at her broken body in the old man's arms one last time before I clicked my magi and walked back to the bar. I didn't even worry about going to the actual bar. I walked right to our room and noticed that she didn't have a single thing left here. Callia was still on the bed, but she was sitting up straight now looking at me with sad eyes.

"It was my fault." I sunk to the floor and pressed my palms into my eyes. "I was a coward."

"*She wouldn't let you rescue her for a reason,*" Callia said.

"I don't believe you." I wiped my nose and shook my head.

"*I don't care. She told me her plans beforehand so I could relay them to you.*" Callia hopped from the bed and pressed her forehead to my fingers.

"*Callia, I need you to do me a favor,*" Shay said from the doorway. "*I need him to know that it isn't his fault. That I need the poison in the blade to set in. He has to be focused on killing me, or he might pull the blade free to properly fight. I never loved Sterling, but I wanted to.*" She looked at the floor and smiled through her pain and tears. "*My things have been sent to Paris already with a note to my family, just in case this doesn't go to plan and I die.*"

Callia pulled away, and I let my head fall back against the wall. She had poisoned him, which meant that if it had sunk in enough, he was weak. If Freya had a chance, it would be now. I needed to get a message to her. Callia gave me a little nod. I pushed open the window, and she turned into a black cat.

"When you get there, change into a dragon and land in the courtyard. You know where to go." I tapped my temple and replayed a map through my mind for her. "Tell her that I am sorry and that I hope I see her when all of this is all said and done."

Callia was gone within seconds.

I TORE my clothes from my body. The suit felt like a prison, and I could no longer handle the events that had unfolded. I went to the little half bath and threw myself into the shower. The water had turned cold long before I had noticed it. My forehead was against the tiled wall when the door opened, and a breeze hit my back. I didn't even move.

"He will not forgive you for having grief over a traitor." A woman's voice spoke up from behind me. I turned around slowly and came face to face with the biggest hair I had ever seen. The woman's dark curly hair was piled high on her head, and she was wearing a crop top and a micro skirt. Did she not realize it was December? I didn't even try to cover myself as I pushed past her and into the room. "You need to pull yourself together if you want to live too."

"Why do you care?" I asked.

"I actually like the witches in this city, and I don't really care for the shell of one that has taken over here. I would like my bar back." The woman crossed her arms and snarled. I could see her canines elongating. No wonder she wasn't cold. She wasn't even human.

"Okay," I muttered as I pulled on some shorts, not wasting time to look for underwear or caring what I looked like now.

"I know you have to grieve your friend, but you must do that at a later date. A war is coming, boy. You better be prepared for it." She folded her arms and shook her head. "You are fixin' to catch a cold. You better put some warm clothes on."

"I'll be fine." I didn't have the strength to say anything else. I didn't know if I could trust her and all I felt was emptiness. I was alone again. Callia wasn't even here to scoff at me.

"Pull yourself together. Cullen will only want the strong to be in his army. He will kill you too if he senses any type of weakness." The woman pulled a bag from under the bed and started to go through it. She pulled out a gray sweater and threw it at my face. I let it slide down me until it crumpled on my lap in a flimsy mess. "You're pathetic."

I knew I was pathetic, but all I could imagine was Freya's life being taken from her in the same manner as Shay. How was someone supposed to remove that from their mind and move on like nothing had happened? I straighten up at the question in my head. I had an answer, and I prayed it was the one thing that would help this mess in my city.

If I was going to survive, I needed to become just as screwed up as Cullen. I needed to become a psychopath too.

CHAPTER TWENTY-SIX

Even though Stark was happily stuck in my brain, something else seemed to be nagging at my mind. The ancestors had been quiet, and the party was now over with. But there was something more. Something was still bothering me. I couldn't quite put my finger on what it was. Tavin followed behind me a few paces, giving me some room and I appreciated it. I wasn't ready to talk about what had transpired between Stark and me.

Stark had taught me valuable things about him and his culture. His people. He taught me about the area he had grown up in and the crime that ran even more rampant there than anywhere else in New Orleans. He had explained so much to me, and my mind was still spinning. But it was what I had wanted. It was what I had needed. If I hadn't listened to the knowledge, I would have continued to leave our coven in a rough place, and I wouldn't be able to help more.

As a coven, we helped our own, but as a person... I knew I needed to do more or at least know more and try to do better. There was only so much I could do for that part of town, but for Stark, I could open doors and possibilities. *Why couldn't he be apart of our coven? Our family? What was wrong with him? A little mortal blood?* I shook my head and tried not to dwell on it much longer. If I didn't watch where I was going, my heel would end up stuck in a drain or worse.

Tavin had offered to take a short cut with me, but I wasn't interested. After the talk with Stark, I needed to see my city with new eyes. I needed to see my town and breathe it all in.

"You're thinking about that boy," Tavin said, directly behind me.

I stumbled in my shoes, and he grabbed my elbow to help steady me. I really didn't want to find myself face down on Bourbon. I threw him an appreciative smile and tried to think of the right thing to say.

People milled all around us, holding their cups of alcohol to the sky.

Drink and be merry for tomorrow you all die…I had thought too soon on the ancestors being gone. Here they were again, full force. *Ugh.*

"Yes, I enjoyed my time with him," I said.

"You were gone for a long time." I knew where he was going with this.

"He taught me a lot."

Tavin stopped and raised his eyebrows at me. "Excuse me?"

Oh, geez, that didn't sound good. I laughed. "I didn't mean it like that, and if I did, it still wouldn't be any of your business. I am a grown *woman.*"

He bowed his head forward in surrender. "Okay, you have a point. What was he educating you on?"

"My city." I left it at that. I still didn't really know my place on all of it or the history of the city, but I needed to tread carefully. There were always listening ears around, especially on the streets of the Quarter.

"Ah, well," He paused and pulled a few of his braids loose. "Sterling was at the party."

I lost my footing entirely at that. I knocked into someone in front of me, that shoved me away from them and hit the concrete hard. The asphalt bit through my dress and into my knees.

I hissed as I realized that my palms had gotten the worst of it. Blood trickled down my hands and onto the ground in front of me. No one stopped to help me, but Tavin leaned down, grabbed me by my elbows once more and hauled me off of the ground.

"Are you all right?" His eyebrows were furrowed, and I could see the pain in his eyes.

"Yes," My dress was already ruined, so I wrapped my bleeding hands in the material around my legs and hoisted the material up, so I didn't trip again. "Continue what you were saying."

"Maybe I should save it for when we are in a safer area. Like maybe your bedroom, where you can't get hurt." He pressed his lips in a thin line and watched the people crowding around us.

"No, go on." I pressed as we pushed through the throng of people on the street.

He sighed. "It's why I disappeared. I wanted to speak to him."

I raised my eyebrows. "Oh, well, okay then."

"I think he is concerned for you and doing dangerous things to keep you safe."

"Good for him," I said. "I don't need a savior."

I marched away from Tavin and hoped he got the hint. Just as we were nearing the coven, he threw his hand up, and the street in front of me tore open and revealed the courtyard. I stepped through and didn't look back.

"He knows that, Freya." He grabbed my hand and pulled me to a halt. I yanked my hand out of his and fixed him with a glare. "He didn't take his eyes off of you once."

"What does that do for me?" I asked, my voice shaking. "Do you know how many times he has left me hanging or how many times he was mean to me? This is just another thing that he does. It's just Sterling and nothing will change him. He can't help it. It's just who he is." I stomped up the stairs, and just as I was about to close the door, I saw Ayre making her way up. Her face was full of pain, and I almost regretted what I had said.

"My brother again? Move on already!" she screamed as I closed the door.

I didn't know if she was saying it to hurt me or because she actually thought I needed to. Or maybe letting out her anger felt better than holding it in.

Vailen had flown out ahead of me, but what I was seeing had me rubbing my eyes. Laying on the bed was Vailen and an all-white dragon. They had their faces pressed together and their eyes closed. I could feel the love in the air and the faint touch of sadness.

"Callia?" I whispered, worried about breaking their special moment. Vailen didn't even open his eyes. He just nodded his head. It was Callia that opened her eyes first. Their crystal blue color pierced through me. "How is this possible? Sterling took your egg with him…"

I ran to the doors and was about to throw them open when Vailen spoke. "*Wait, he isn't here.*"

I skidded to a stop and closed my eyes. After what I had just said about him, I probably didn't deserve him anyway.

"*I'll show you all you need to know.*" He paused. "*Then we go to war.*"

CHAPTER TWENTY-SEVEN

STERLING

I listened to the yelling downstairs, and I knew he was coming for me next. I could feel it in my bones, and it didn't help that my magi was scorching my chest. I laid in the dark with my eyes closed. I was exceptionally still, given the circumstances. When the door opened and shined a light on me, it wasn't Cullen in the doorway. It was a Vampire that I hadn't met before. His sickly white skin gave him away.

"Get up." I did as he said and got up from the bed. All I wore was sweat pants, and when I went to grab my shirt, the monster held his hand up. "What you have on is fine."

I nodded my head and followed him down the stairs. Cullen's face had hatred written all over it when he turned my way. "You returned her to her coven!" he roared. He threw his beer bottle across the room, and it burst when it hit the wall. The golden liquid splashed the floor and Cullen spit.

"I didn't think there was anything wrong with that. Doesn't she deserve to be with her people?" I asked.

"I underestimated your feelings for her. Do you know what happens when you return the body of a witch to her family?" Cullen asked.

"Her spirit is allowed to rest with the ancestors," I answered.

"Yes, and her magic goes back to the coven." He snarled. "You didn't get her magi, did you?"

I shook my head. "I didn't realize I was one of your henchmen."

Cullen laughed, but it was empty. "Jax, take him in the pit and teach him a lesson that he will never forget. Don't stop until he's broken."

I put my hand over my magi and was about to fight, but someone put a sack over my head and was already using magic to keep me from doing much. I could feel its substantial effects on me.

Cullen whispered in my ear just as they were yanking me away. "Everyone that serves me is a henchman. You won't forget it again."

. . .

CULLEN'S WORDS echoed in my mind as I was stretched out on a table. My magi felt like it was going to burn a hole through my chest.

"Should we rip his magi from him?" someone asked.

I bucked off the table. My wrists were shackled down with magic inhibitor handcuffs, and I was going to burn myself out if I kept up with my fight. A man across the room cackled. "Tough guy can't hang."

I sucked oxygen in through my nose and tried to keep it together. All I could see was blackness, and the musty smell of the fabric was churning my stomach.

"I just want a taste," someone else said. "Jax, just let us have a little taste."

"Absolutely not. We aren't here for a snack. We are here to break his soul." Jax said. Something crashed against the wall, and I heard all of the others whimper before the door slammed closed. "Where were we?"

I bucked off the table again, hoping I could get my foot loose and do some damage.

"Ah, that's right." He tsked. "Getting this little fire in you to go out."

The scraping of metal against metal made me

freeze.

"Got your attention, I see." The table under me vibrated as he ran something down it. I held my breath when I felt him press the blade into the bottom of my foot. My magi protected me from most of the pain, but I could still feel how deep it was going into my flesh.

I clenched my jaw and tried not to move when he went to the other foot. Once again my magi protected me from the brunt of it. There was a grunt of frustration, and I heard metal clang against the wall. He had thrown the knife.

"I will break you. You think you are tough and you think you can handle this," he shouted. "I will make you scream."

He continued for hours, pulling my skin back and trying new methods before he turned me over and began to carve on my back. I could feel my magi starting to lose its fight and soon the magic was gone and I could feel it all. The pain came rushing to me like I had been hit by a train with no warning.

The blade dug deeper into my back, and I bit down as hard as I could on the fabric around my face. I didn't know how it had gotten close enough for me to do it, but I was thankful. He tossed the knife on the table next to my face and walked away. I let out the breath of air I had been holding, but then his footsteps started to head back my way.

Blinding white pain. My eyes were closed, and white flashed across my vision. I let out a shaky breath, and then the whip snapped again, and I waited for its excruciating decent once more. I hissed between my teeth when it made contact with my raw and bleeding back. He snapped it again, and I let out a scream of agony.

"Mercy." Jax taunted. "Beg for mercy." I would never beg for anything from this man. I gritted my teeth and waited for the whip to fly again.

I HAD BEEN GONE from the pain for hours it seemed. I had passed out, and the only thing that had woken me was the other henchmen ripping the sack off of my head. My head pitched forward and then slammed back onto the metal table. I groaned and tried to close my eyes tighter. The light was even more torture on my poor deprived eyes.

"Get up now." The woman in front of me commanded.

I opened my eyes in shock. I didn't know how

they thought I was going to be able to do that. I frowned at her.

"If you don't get up, someone out there, will come in here and throw you off," she said softer.

I nodded my head and scooted to the edge of the table. When my feet touched the floor, the fire ignited through my legs. There were burns around my ankles from the shackles that had kept my magic in.

"Your injuries are extensive." She muttered something else that I couldn't understand under her breath.

"Yeah," I grunted out.

"I am not allowed to treat you." She paused. "But I will do what I can to help you and keep you strong. I don't enjoy this part of my loyalty."

"It's very apparent that you are all mindless creatures." I didn't care if I hurt her, or if what I said would get me more time down here. I was dead, no matter what I did. Cullen would eventually find out where my loyalties lied and he would off me.

"That's not true," she whispered.

"Then prove it to me."

She shook her head, and her blonde hair made a wave around her face. "I'll see what I can do."

Freya

THE SCREAMING WOKE ME UP. I shot up in bed and looked around me frantically in the dark. I pushed my hair from my face and tried to locate the noise. I snapped my fingers and whispered, "*Illumiá!*" A soft glow illuminated the room from my fingertips. Liam had put together a small book, that I kept under my pillow, of small spells to help me get used to practicing magic. Some of them were trickier than others, but this one was the first I had memorized. I hated having to get my cellphone out to use the flashlight option on it.

Callia was sitting up from the floor, terror all over her dragon features. Smoke was rising from her nostrils, and Vailen was rubbing his face against her neck.

"What's the matter? What happened?" I asked, throwing the covers away from my legs to fall from the bed.

"*Sterling,*" Vailen stopped. "*He is in danger.*"

Callia shook her head at him, her eyes squeezed shut. "*He is being tortured.*"

I was grateful I was already on the floor, or I

would have ended up face down. I pressed my fingers into the cold floor and tried to breathe. Tavin had given me hope. Sterling had been there, and he had risked it all for me. Even though I had said such hurtful things. I didn't know if I meant all of them.

My French doors burst open, and there was Tavin, oddly enough, with a sword raised high, ready to take down anything. The sword glinted lavender in the light coming off of my fingers.

"What was that noise?" he asked.

"Callia." I let out a breath to steady myself. No one needed me panicking. I could see Ayre and Liam standing behind my father, and I knew I needed to keep it as calm as I could. If not for the coven, but for my best friend. "She is bonded to Sterling, at least we hope all the way, and she's experiencing his memories and his… pain."

Ayre shoved Tavin out of her way and fell to Callia's side. "Please, please tell me that my brother is okay."

Callia closed her eyes, got up and walked away from all of us. Vailen gave me sad eyes. *"She doesn't understand what is happening. His thoughts and memories are coming in a jumbled mess. She can feel his pain though, and it's tearing her apart."* He stretched out like a feline and followed her. He stopped before he got to the windows that were now open. "*She is regretting leaving him. She knows they don't have a strong bond emotionally, but he is her human all the same.*"

CHAPTER TWENTY-EIGHT

FREYA

Callia no longer felt Sterling. Whatever had been tethering them together was now gone.

I, of course, feared the worst and so did Ayre, but what was I supposed to do? I couldn't march into battle unprepared and all for one man. Even though that man meant much to our coven. I ran a comb through my wet, matted hair and watched my two dragons laying in the warmth of the sunlight streaming through the windows. Vailen had been silent since everything had happened a few nights prior.

Ayre lounged in the chair and watched me, sadness and curiosity mixing on her face. "What are we going to do?"

"We are going to have to wait it out. I know you don't like that and I know you will object, but I don't know what else I am supposed to do." I threw the comb against the wall. It bounced off and skidded under the bed, almost as if it was mocking me too.

Ayre nodded her head and said, "Okay, fair enough. I wouldn't know what to do either. Many of the coven saw you that night. They saw what happened when you got off of Vailen's back. I saw them hiding in the shadows. They would die for you if you marched them to war. They know what this monster did."

"Yes, but for what? One man? One man that we don't even know if he's alive?"

Ayre clenched her jaw and tears filled her eyes. A few spilled over, but the rest she blinked away. "They would die for Sterling too. They grew up with him, helped raise him. He was The High Priestess' son at one point."

"I care about him too!" I stood up and pinched the bridge of my nose. "You forget that! You forget that I thought of a future with him. I imagined things that I was scared of. He battled for me, like a little jealous imp, in The Mirror Realm. I don't forget everything he has done for me."

Ayre was opening her mouth to say something when there was a knock on the door. She was probably going to remind me of the things I had said to Tavin, remarks I had made when I was hurt and deflecting. Jonathan pushed the doors open and gave me a severe look. "We have a meeting with The Council."

I frowned. I didn't remember having anything scheduled, but then again, The Council did what they wanted, when they wanted. The didn't abide by a calendar.

I pushed my long hair into a ponytail and followed him out of my room. I paused at the doorway and looked back at my best friend. "I promise you, on my life and my magic, that I will do what it takes to get him back. I swear to you that I will fight for him, like no other." Ayre closed her eyes and bowed her head forward.

Jonathan was waiting for me at the stairs. He gave me a severe look. "That is a serious promise, and your magi will have to hold you to it."

"I know, Liam wrote it in my book that he gave me," I said.

"That was very thoughtful of him," Jonathan muttered.

"I guess. I think he did it because he has pity

for me that my teacher abandoned me." I shrugged, trying to not let my words have too much emotion.

"You're about to have more answers about that in a moment." He pushed the door open to the study, and it was just like last time. The Council all stood in a line, waiting for me to join them. "Wait here," Jonathan told me as he made his way to the line. My father was all the way at the end, wearing his rebellious attire. His tattoos on proud display. He bowed his head to me in acknowledgment as I faced off with all of them.

The man that Jonathan had called Leaf stepped forward. He had a black suit on and from the state of his face, he had been crying. "I am here to report a death."

The suspense would literally kill me. My eyes flicked to Jonathan. His face was void of all emotion. I could feel my body starting to shake with adrenaline. I dreaded the worst and couldn't bear to hear what he was going to say next.

"My daughter, Shay," He stopped. "was murdered. She was next in line to be The High Priestess of the Paris coven." His eyes landed on me, and he snarled. "Murdered by your brother."

Jonathan stepped forward. "That's enough." He

put his hand on Leaf's shoulder. "Tell us what her magi read."

Leaf blinked, and it was like he had turned into a new person. "She was working with Sterling Masters to bring down Cullen, or as we thought we knew him, Axel. She stabbed him with a poison blade, and he strangled her to death, while Sterling stood and watched. Though, she didn't want him to try to save her."

Some whispers erupted around the room. The Council members talked amongst themselves, while I stood there like I, quite naturally, didn't belong. While they spoke, I let my mind wander and didn't worry with what they were saying. If they wanted to include me, they would.

Except they didn't. They were interrupted by screaming. I pushed through them all to get out of the door and to the courtyard where the commotion was coming from. The entire way I was having flashbacks, but what was happening now was much worse than what had happened that night.

Bodies littered the courtyard. I couldn't count just how many. There was blood and gore everywhere I turned and more kept popping in. Old and young were laid out in front of me. I couldn't tell if these were casualties or they were alive.

There was gasp behind me, but I didn't turn around to see who it was that had made the noise. I ran to the first child and checked for a pulse at her neck. It was still there, but weak. Where were the healers? Couldn't they hear the screaming and wailing?

Jonathan ran past me and started to administer to the rest of the injured and dying. The rest of The Council recovered from their shock and did the same. A little girl that had claw marks down her face ran to me. I grabbed her in my arms and pressed her face into my shirt.

"What happened?" I hoped that I would get some type of answer.

"Rougarou!"

It was broad daylight. Jonathan looked up at me from a body with a frown on his face. He had heard her and was just as confused as I was. The last attack had been at night. This made no sense. But then again, neither did the mad man that had orchestrated this. I knew in my heart that it was Cullen. Who else would inflict this kind of damage? Who else was this evil?

Sariah was many things, and she had done some harm, but this? I knew that she wasn't capable of this. She had turned to dark magic to save children, her own children, but children all the same. She wouldn't kill them for no purpose.

I tore the sleeves of my shirt off and pressed the material to the little girls face. She was shaking from either the cold or shock, so I wrapped my arms around her again. I held onto the other child lying beside us and hoped that more healers were on their way. Though, we didn't have enough healers for something like this, did we?

I PACED THE HALLWAY. The infirmary was maxed out, and there were people wherever we could get them. There were four to five victims to a room and a few in the hall with me, the ones that didn't have as extensive injuries.

Twenty-nine dead. All of their magis ripped off. We still didn't have a count on the injured, but most of them would soon join the dead, their magis had also been removed, and they wouldn't survive long without them. A sob tore it's way up my throat, and I had to excuse myself from the hallway. I couldn't be strong enough for my people.

Ayre caught me on the way out and pulled me in for a hug. She held onto me as my body shook with the sobs. My best friend held onto me as I fell apart, right there in the wide open and she didn't let me go. She kept me together for just a few brief seconds that felt like a lifetime until I could pull away and wipe my face clean.

"This isn't something that I want to tell you, but now that you have let it out, there's more." She wiped her own cheeks and frowned.

"Isn't there always? Isn't there always something more when we think we can't go any farther?" I held back more tears.

"There are four rougarou in the Quarter. There were twelve."

Hope blossomed in my chest. "That's good then."

She tilted her head. "Yes, but our people are out there battling them."

I realized what she was saying. Ayre continued, "There will be more. Cullen will create more."

"Has anyone spoken to The Hebert Coven and made sure that all their wolves are accounted for or maybe they need to go on lockdown?" I asked.

Ayre shrugged. "I don't know, but you need a shower and to take a break. You have been here for hours, and you have blood all over you."

"I can't leave my people." I protested.

"Your people need you strong. I need you

strong. Sterling needs you strong. You can't be strong by being here right now. Know that your people are in good hands. Check on Vailen and Callia, I know they weren't doing well with all the blood and emotions in the air." She grabbed my shoulder and pulled me in for another hug. "Take care of you. You can't pour from an empty cup."

"When did you get so wise?" I asked.

All she did was smile and shove me through the doorway.

VAILEN AND CALLIA were curled up sleeping when I pushed my door open, like two cats. At the thought, Vailen picked his head up and glared at me. Maybe not sleeping. His eyes became slits before he curled up against his mate again.

I pressed my forehead against the cold tile wall and let the water rush down my back. I didn't worry about washing my hair or cleaning myself. There was a pull inside my soul, and I couldn't pinpoint the feeling. I imagined the feeling like Vailen had taught me with my magic and reached out for it. When I touched it, I was snapped backward and hit the opposite wall of the shower. As much as it had hurt me, I went to reach for it again. That same pull grabbed at my mind again, this time I touched it hesitantly.

I gasped. Sterling was laying on a bloodied bed. I looked around to make sure that we were alone before I rushed to his side. His eyes barely opened, and his lips turned up slightly in a painful smile then his face turned to dread.

"What are you doing here?" he whispered.

"I don't know, but I don't think that I am actually here. I was in the shower, and I'm fully clothed now. I think we are somehow mind-sharing." I shrugged.

"That couldn't be possible."

I remembered Callia and Vailen curled up. "I think our familiars are making this happen for us."

He closed his eyes and fell back onto the pillow. The redness on the sheets underneath him was growing.

"What do I do?" I asked, frantically.

"You can't do anything if this isn't real."

"I am going to try." I helped him roll onto his stomach and peeled the material from his bloodied back. It made a sickly noise, and it pulled loose from the skin. What the material revealed had me covering my mouth in horror. Long, deep gouges of skin were taken from his back, and there were various other marks spread out on the surface of his shoulders.

I did the only thing I could think of. As I pressed my palms against his back, he hissed through his teeth. I wanted to be gentle, but I knew there was no time for that. There had been too much destruction for our coven, I would be pulled back to reality soon. I closed my eyes and imagined the red energy inside of me, my magi, and pushed it from my hands. I thought of his back repairing its-self and the blood going away. I imagined my magic destroying any bacteria or germs in his cuts. I pushed more and more into it until I was getting lightheaded.

"Stop," he croaked out. "You can't go like this."

When I opened my eyes, I staggered backward and almost fell to the floor. Most of the cuts were healed, and the skin looked like it was starting to stitch back everywhere else.

"I have to keep going. You are almost healed." I rushed forward.

Sterling shook his head, his matted hair lifting from his forehead with the movement. "And when they come back?"

"Then I will heal you again!" I insisted.

"You are too stubborn for your own good." He

pushed me away. "Something happened today. I could sense it."

"Cullen sent out an attack against the coven, and Shay's father rallied The Council," I said.

"Good, there is going to be a war," he said.

"Not good. What about you?" I asked.

"I don't know, they're trying to break me, and they might succeed." Sterling looked at the ground, and that was when I noticed how hollow his face looked. He was regaining some color, but only because of my magic I had pushed into him. He wouldn't last much longer.

"I will make sure that they don't." It was like no time had passed between us. It was like he hadn't left to begin with and we were picking up right where we had left off.

"Your father is pretty badass."

I laughed and rolled my eyes, trying to not get distracted by Sterling changing the subject. "Yeah, he would like to think so."

"You get it from him."

"Whatever," I smirked. Then the pull happened again, but this time it was away from Sterling. I frowned and grabbed his face between my hands. I pressed a quick peck on his lips and went to pull away. I was too slow, and Sterling grabbed me and pulled me back to him. His lips crushed against mine and when he pulled away, I was breathing hard and trying to remember the mission at hand.

"Whatever happens, defeat Cullen. Do not try to save me. I am one man, and my life isn't of much importance. When it comes down to it, kill me if you have to. Cullen has too many plans for New Orleans to lose you. I am nothing."

Just as the last words left his mouth, I was ripped from his arms and thrust back into my body. Icy cold water was splashing my back, but I didn't feel it. Ayre was standing in the doorway holding a towel, looking concerned.

"How long have I been like this?" I asked as I took the towel out of her hands.

"Maybe an hour."

"There's no way," I said.

"I've been standing here for a while." She huffed. "I tried to get answers from the dragon, but all he did was roll his eyes. Why did Sterling have to get the cool dragon too? Why couldn't I have gotten one? It would have been much easier to communicate if I had the keys here."

Familiars aren't forever… The ancestors whispered around me.

CHAPTER TWENTY-NINE

STERLING

I woke up with a start and sat up straight in the bed, which shouldn't have been possible with my injuries. I rubbed my eyes.

Freya.

She had been right there in my dreams, and she had seemed so real. Her wet hair hanging over her shoulders in loose waves. She had been a dream come true. I drew my hands down my face and exhaled.

"You seem to be feeling much better." Someone new said from the doorway. This one I didn't recognize. They would probably continue to send more Vampires until they were able to break me.

I didn't say anything.

He stalked toward me and pulled the sheet from

my back. It had stuck to the blood there and dried to my back. I tried not to wince at the new wounds he was creating by doing that. "Well, looks like you heal a lot better than what we thought."

He curled his lip and me and out a whistle that was long and shrill. The room was quickly flooded with Vampires. Their canines elongated, and they started to hum in unison. I closed my eyes and waited for the piercing pain.

It was worse than I could have ever imagined. My mother had always warned us that it was better to have Vampires as friends, rather than enemies. With their lips and teeth on my body, I now thoroughly understood. At the Institute they had said a feeding was a sensual experience. They described it as seduction, and many of the witches in the classroom had blushed.

This was nothing like they had described. In the back of my mind, I barely remembered the professors speak on the involuntary feedings and that they could be painful. This was beyond painful. This was worse than the whipping. It felt like little needles all over my body that were caught on fire. Every sip of blood they took was lava in my veins. The pain was so immense, I felt myself starting to fade. No sounds escaped my lips, no cries of agony or terror.

I was just there, floating above it all, eventually numb.

EVENTUALLY, the door creaked open, but I didn't know what was happening at that point. I was too high from the pain and the toxins they were pumping into my body. My head lolled uselessly to the side, and my eyes were just slightly open, trying to stay alive. Though I didn't know how I was still there.

"What do you think you are doing?!" Cullen roared from the doorway. The pain at the back of my mind receded.

Someone answered, but I couldn't make out who through the haze. "We are breaking him like you ordered."

"This is not breaking! This is killing! Did I say that I wanted him dead?" Cullen was eerily calm, that was apparent from the sound of his voice.

"What would you like us to do, Master?"

"Heal him and don't do this shit again." He slammed the door behind him, and the thin wall rattled.

I heard someone hiss and the sound of someone biting into flesh. I was too far gone to know if it was mine or not. It didn't matter, I was still here, somehow.

Something was pressed against my lips and liquid spilled into my mouth. The taste was horrendous, but I didn't have the strength to pull away. The noxious substance continued to drip past my lips. My strength returned, and I was able to open my eyes all the way. A Vampire's wrist was pressed to my mouth, and I was drinking from her. I pulled my head away and noticed something weird in her eyes.

Sympathy.

"Don't look at me like that. You of all should know that you can't be turned," she said. She flicked her dark hair over her shoulder and reminded me of Shay. I tried to push the pain away with the thought. She was here to hurt me emotionally. I tried to not be paranoid, but that was the only way to be now.

I raised my lip in disgust. "I know that."

I felt like a new man, but at the thought, my stomach rolled. I couldn't believe that I had drunk from the parasite its self. My mouth felt dry, and I found myself frowning.

"By Merlin! You are all right!" Callia's voice filled my head. I could see a picture of her in standing next to Vailen, but what was in front of them had me remembering my conversation with Freya. Bodies littered the courtyard, and I couldn't tell if they were alive or dead.

The door opened back up, and Cullen had a massive grin on his face. "I have learned that your little familiar has escaped." I looked at his soulless eyes and spit at his feet. He laughed. "I see that you still haven't learned anything."

"How is a person supposed to learn from torture?" I asked.

"I do see that it did the opposite of what was intended." Cullen frowned, then he shrugged. "No matter, I will just have to show you why everyone here fears me. I will have to show you true power. Power from the Gods, power from Merlin, and not your silly little essence."

A yre held my hands in hers and pulled me in for a hug. "Are you sure you're ready for this?"

I looked down at Vailen and Callia and nodded my head. This war was going to be over before it started. The Master's stood behind me with the rest of the coven. Everyone but Sterling. I would have been lying to say that I didn't miss him. Our last conversation was still fresh in my mind.

Tavin stood right next to me, ready to defend me no matter the cost. I wondered if Sariah would bail on us or actually show up and right her wrongs. Tavin straightened his leather coat and popped his neck. He crunched his knuckles and gave me a loaded look. A look full of hope and sadness and I knew my face mirrored his. I looked down at my leathers and sent up a prayer to the essence and the ancestors. I didn't know what was going to go down, but I needed it all on my side. On our side.

I needed as much good juju as we could muster.

We walked through our magic portal, or whatever it was called. Ayre kept saying it was Air Walking, but it sounded weird coming from her so I pushed it aside and called it weird things until I could get the hang of it.

The air wavered in front of us, and we stepped through it confidently. The night was dark, and there was a fog settling in around us. I knew this wasn't just a coincidence. The grass was slick but didn't make a noise as we walked inward.

I bit my lip when I saw him. His hair and skin matched mine, but his eyes... his eyes were dead and gone, black pits in his face. He smiled like he hadn't killed me, and took a few steps forward. He was wearing a biker get up, and he was shirtless under his black vest. The witches that followed him through the fog were strangers until the last one stepped up. Right behind Sterling came the Vampires, we had some on our side. It was undeniable of what they were, simply by the way they walked. But no matter how many people came through the fog, my mind was stuck on one.

Sterling.

His face held no emotion as he looked at all of us like he was gone. He had sent the warning with his dragon, he had been tortured and drained but had still been strong enough for Callia to get through to him one last time, but whatever had happened after that had changed him for the worst.

He resembled a shell, just like Cullen. His clothing didn't even match him. All black and biker to the T. He wouldn't look in my direction, and I imagined that was a good thing. There was only so much I could take of all of this, especially as I faced the brother I was just now starting to remember. We had history, and I wished we didn't. It would make things complicated. I could feel it in my soul that this would be too long of a night.

"Hello, sister. We meet again." Cullen was the first to speak.

"Brother. This ends tonight." I said, even though, I knew this wouldn't be the end. It had to start somewhere. I rushed forward and let my magic do the rest of the talking.

ACKNOWLEDGMENTS

Just like that, another book quickly finished. I can hardly believe it. I can hardly believe that we did it! Again, there are so many that I HAVE/NEED to thank.

Starting with my husband for all of the late nights letting me talk endlessly about all of this, even though, he has no idea about any of it. Also, for putting Mason to bed each night and giving me the time for myself to do with what I please. I am eternally grateful for you and all that you do to make my passions and dreams possible.

Tori- for literally fan girling over anything and everything that I write! You seriously are the only reason this series exists! You believe in me and help me more than you know. Thank you for letting me blow you phone up when I'm writing. Thank you for letting me annoy you and thank you for continuing to push me!

My reviewers and readers!!! Y'all seriously make all of this possible. I would be nothing without each of you. Thank you for being fans and loving me, even when I feel my work is terrible and not good enough! Thank you for being so awesome!

ABOUT THE AUTHOR

A. Lonergan lives in her own world. She doesn't let anyone tell her what to do, except MAYBE her 4 year old. She loves fiercely and enjoys writing stories with heart and passion, but also a little pain. She wants her readers to feel like she does as she writes. She believes that there is nothing more powerful than being able to make someone feel something. You can catch up with her on any and all platforms below, feel free to reach out! She loves to meet new people!

COMING SOON LATE SUMMER OF 2019!
BOOK 3 IN THE WITCHES OF JACKSON
SQUARE SERIES, CAPTIVATED.

Chapter 1

Freya

We exchanged spar for spar. Every move I had, my brother seemed to know before I did. Sweat was starting to roll down my face, but I continued to push myself. I could hear my people crying out from the battlefield around us, and I couldn't allow their sacrifices to be in vain. Lightning shot from my hands and took Cullen by surprise. The sudden blow had him gasping for air.

"Surrender," I said as I stepped on his chest. I pressed down with the toe of my boot. "I said, surrender, Cullen."

"I will do no such thing." He made a waving motion, and I was thrown from his body. I hit a tree with a loud snap and rolled to the ground, twigs cutting into my skin on the way down. "You see, you don't realize my power. None of your little kinfolks do."

I coughed and rolled to my stomach before he got to me. He took his sweet time, watching me with a sick expression on his face. "Though, I will admit that you intrigue me."

I flicked my fingers forward on my side, and a tree branch came down and wrapped around him like a rope. "Good, keep talking." I laughed as the branch continued to curl around his body and eventually covered up his mouth. His breathing became more labored as the branch tightened. "This was almost too easy."

I heard a cry of pain from my father and I whipped around. He was on the ground, and a Vampire had him pinned. The Vampire was beginning to drink from him. I pulled my hand toward the sky with my palm open, and roots impaled the woman. Tavin, my father, fell backward onto the grass and gave me an appreciative smile before he jumped back into battle.

"You are a powerful witch. You could be more." Cullen said.

I turned around and faced him again, keeping myself aware of my surroundings at the same time. He was still in my trees clutches, but I didn't know just how long it would hold him. I hadn't practiced my magic like this before.

Yes, you could be more... I sighed at the constant call of the ancestors in my mind. They would be there until I had a daughter that would take the torch from me and I was still pretty sure, I would get their daily reminders even then.

"You know nothing about me." I could hear a Vampire approaching me, and I pulled my hand down, forming a fist. A branch came down, similar to the one holding Cullen, but this one shot through the man's chest. He pitched forward, and his mouth gaped open. In the morning, when the sun shone on his remains, he would turn to dust. They all would. Cullen had to know that the sunrise would be coming soon.

Knowing him, he had a backup plan. He was too smart not to.

"What do you want?" I asked, again. I had been asking him it all night. He had evaded me in any way he could. I didn't want to hurt my brother, even though he had succeeded in killing me.

"I want you dead." His words pierced my heart. I had known this. I had reminded myself of this daily, but it still didn't lessen the blow.

Every time we paused, I would get a flashback. Each one was just as painful as the first.

"Come and get me, Frey!" Cullen taunted me. His bright green eyes shining as he ran from me. We had been staying at The Hebert's Coven, in hopes that the fresh air would help Cullen's magic manifest and that his sickness would leave. Mother had been sure to keep it a secret, but I wasn't dumb. I could see my brother hacking up blood, and his random nose-bleeds didn't seem so random anymore. Ma Agata scolded him again and gave me a look. She had a switch on the kitchen counter, and I knew she would use it on me.

She wouldn't use it on Cullen, he was too weak, but she always used me for his punishments, and he would listen then. He hated to see me in pain.

This memory was the longest and the most painful. I swallowed back the tears and wondered what had happened. Why did he hate me so? What had I done to deserve his wrath?

Enjoyed what you read? It makes A. Lonergan do happy dances when her readers leave reviews! Please consider doing that for her as a "thank you" for writing this novel for your enjoyment! The more reviews she can get, the faster she will write!

64943173R00159

Made in the USA
Middletown, DE
06 September 2019